"What gives women the right to assume so much?"

"Assume? Like what?"

"Like imagining they can take up where they left off," he gritted.

"Somebody is doing that?" Lucy queried innocently, her mind darting to the perfumed letter Silas had just received.

"It would appear to be so."

Miriam MacGregor began writing under the tutelage of a renowned military historian, and produced articles and books—fiction and nonfiction—concerning New Zealand's pioneer days, as well as plays for a local drama club. In 1984, she received an award for her contribution to New Zealand's literary field. She now writes romance novels exclusively and derives great pleasure from offering readers escape from everyday life. She and her husband live on a sheep-and-cattle station near the small town of Waipawa.

Books by Miriam MacGregor

WILDER'S WILDERNESS
Miriam MacGregor

Harlequin Books

TORONTO • NEW YORK • LONDON
AMSTERDAM • PARIS • SYDNEY • HAMBURG
STOCKHOLM • ATHENS • TOKYO • MILAN
MADRID • WARSAW • BUDAPEST • AUCKLAND

ISBN 0-373-17172-2

WILDER'S WILDERNESS

Copyright © 1993 by Miriam MacGregor.

Printed in U.S.A.

CHAPTER ONE

Lucy Telford drove at a steady pace, her mind occupied by the task set for her by Aunt Bertha. It was a task that nagged at her, the mere thought of it causing a furrow to crease her normally smooth brow. Why hadn't she the strength to stand against her aunt's demands? she wondered, not for the first time.

The route was taking her over a highway that twisted and turned across central North Island mountain ranges where the air was fresh and clear. The September sun, proclaiming early spring in New Zealand, cast shadows between the millions of pine trees planted to cover hills that had become wasteland after the removal of native bush. Row upon row they seemed to march, reminding Lucy of soldiers dressed in Prussian green uniforms.

Suddenly her attention was caught by the sight of a light utility truck parked on the roadside a short distance ahead—and as she drew nearer a man stepped from behind it and held up his hand. She removed her foot from the accelerator, checked that the doors were locked, then stopped the red Toyota beside him. As she did so she noticed a second man, who peered with interest from the passenger seat of the utility.

The tall man who spoke to her through the barely opened driver's window was casually dressed in a well-cut tweed sports jacket and green drill trousers. His broad shoulders and narrow hips spoke of virility, while his tanned complexion indicated an outdoor life. When he spoke, his deep voice held a vibrancy that drew attention.

'I've run out of petrol,' he explained. 'Can you give me a lift to beyond the Mohaka River?'

She looked at the handsome features framed by thick, straight dark hair, and into a pair of brown eyes set beneath dark brows. My goodness, he's attractive, she thought. And then, with the force of a hurled dart, her mother's words shot into her mind. On the day Lucy had been presented with the key of the Toyota, Margaret Telford had said, 'Now promise me you'll never pick up hitch-hikers or strangers. Ghastly things have happened to girls who have been stupid enough to do so.'

And Lucy had promised; therefore she now said, 'I'm sorry—I promised my mother I'd never pick up people I don't know.'

The man drew a hissing breath of impatience as he gritted, 'Tell your mother it's imperative for me to reach the other side of the river. It's only a few miles further along the road.'

'I would if she were here,' Lucy retorted. 'But don't worry, another car is sure to come quite soon. You'll get there eventually—but not with me.'

The man's gaze raked her clear complexion and pale gold hair, then his mouth twisted slightly as he drawled in a sardonic tone, 'What's the matter, Cornflower? Are you afraid of me?'

Her brows rose as she glared at him. '*Cornflower*. . .?'

'I've never seen such deep blue eyes.'

'Really? I'm afraid compliments will get you nowhere.'

'For Pete's sake give me a lift. You'd be quite safe, I assure you. I don't go for blondes. Only brunettes.'

A flush stole into Lucy's cheeks as she snapped coldly, 'In that case, better luck next time.' Her foot moved from the brake to the accelerator and the car glided forward.

Small as it was, the incident disturbed her, perhaps because there had been something about the man that had appealed to her. It was almost as if he'd reached out to clasp her hand in his plea for help, and she knew she'd wanted to give him a lift. But then, coupled with the promise made to her mother, common sense had prevailed to remind her that unpleasant experiences had been known to result from giving lifts to strangers.

Vaguely irritated, she decided to blame Aunt Bertha for the incident, because it was on her account that she was here at this particular time. Nor would it have occurred if her aunt had not written several gloomy letters to Mother—letters that had been full of pathos and self-pity.

When the last one had arrived at their home in Wellington, Margaret Telford had said thoughtfully to Lucy, 'There's something wrong with Bertha. She's not her usual aggressive self. She's depressed—and that's not like Bertha. I'll ask Daddy to give you a few days off from the office. I'd be grateful if you'd go to Hastings to see if you can discover what's niggling at her. It'll give you a nice little break from the typewriter.'

Lucy had felt dismayed. 'If you don't mind, Mother, I'd prefer to deal with the typewriter. It's not full of criticisms!'

'My dear, your aunt Bertha *means* well——'

'Does she, indeed? Then why don't you go? She's *your* sister and it would give you a break. It's time you had one.'

Her mother's excuse had come readily. 'My dear, you know I have Daddy to care for, as well as Gran. She hasn't been well, and I wouldn't dream of leaving her until she's really over her last bout of bronchitis.'

Reluctantly, Lucy had packed a small suitcase and had driven the four-hour journey to Hastings, a city situated in the centre of the fertile Heretuanga plains of Hawke's Bay, where fruit and vegetables grew in abundance. Nor had it taken her long to discover the source of her aunt's woes, and now the reason for them returned to her mind.

'Of course it's *Silas*,' Bertha had exclaimed irritably within five minutes of Lucy's arrival at the large house nestling among trees and gardens in the most expensive area of Hastings. 'You know Silas, my stepson——' Her grey eyes had flashed in anger.

'No, Aunt, I don't know Silas. I've never met him,' Lucy had reminded her patiently.

'He was fourteen when I married his father, and that's twenty years ago—which makes him thirty-four years of age now.'

'Ten years older than me,' Lucy had mused.

Bertha's voice had quivered with indignation. 'He's old enough to have respect for one who cared for him during his teenage years. Didn't I attend to his clothes, cook his meals——?'

'But, Aunt, he was only a boy,' Lucy had protested. 'As his stepmother, wouldn't it have been expected of you?'

The question had been ignored. 'And after all I've done for him—he's *deserted* me. He hasn't been near me for *three years.*' Bertha had drawn a deep breath before adding vehemently, 'And as for that woman, *Doreen*—she was really at the base of our quarrel.'

'Who is Doreen?'

'A—a *female* he was almost engaged to. I trust they're not now *living in sin.*'

'Tell me about the quarrel,' Lucy had urged, making an effort to clear the situation in her mind.

'It was bitter,' Bertha had admitted. 'I'm afraid I lost my temper. I told him I hoped I'd *never see him again*——'

'In that case you can't say he's deserted you. He's given you your wish by keeping away,' Lucy had reasoned.

Bertha had looked at her in thoughtful silence for several long moments before she'd said, '*Dear* Lucy—I believe you could help me in this affair.'

'What do you mean?' A determined glint in her aunt's eye had caused Lucy to become aware of a sudden misgiving. Nor had she the slightest desire to become involved in her aunt's quarrel. 'I can't see how I can possibly help you,' she had said firmly.

'Yes, you can. You can go to Silas for me. I've been told he left the accountancy firm where he worked, and that he's joined his uncle, Matthew Wilder, who owns a back-country property between Napier and Taupo. I believe there's a road leading to it a short distance beyond the Mohaka River bridge.' She paused reflectively. 'My dear Tom spoke of the place as an undeveloped shambles with Matt living there alone, although I've now heard that he and Silas accommodate a few guests. The place is known as Wilder's Wilderness.'

Lucy had looked at her aunt in puzzled silence before saying, 'No doubt I could find this place—but what on earth do you expect me to do when I get there?'

'You can *talk* to him for me, my dear. You can tell him that *all is forgiven* and that I—I want him to come and visit me.'

'That should give him a good laugh.' Lucy had been unable to disguise her own amusement.

'He should have *known* I didn't mean the things I said,' Bertha had persisted stubbornly. 'After all, he's Tom's son and I do want to see him again. It was only *that Doreen* I wanted out of my sight.'

'What makes you imagine he'll listen to me?' Lucy had queried doubtfully. 'Remember, I'm a complete stranger to him.'

'It's what you say that will have the effect. You can tell him it is what his father would have wished him to do.' Bertha had sat back with the satisfied air of having played a trump card, until suddenly her lip had quivered as tears filled her eyes. 'Poor Tom would have been so very unhappy if he'd known of this situation,' she'd sniffed while fumbling for a handkerchief.

Lucy had regarded her aunt searchingly. 'I think the

solution is simple. All you have to do is drive to this
place and hold out a hand in friendship.'

Bertha had looked affronted as she'd drawn herself to
her full height. 'You're suggesting that I go to *him?*'
she'd hissed. 'Certainly not. *He* must come to *me*.'

Despite the hardness of her aunt's attitude, the latter's
distress had got through to Lucy, causing her to become
engulfed with sympathy for the older woman. And there
lay the reason she was now driving towards Wilder's
Wilderness. What her reception would be she feared to
imagine, and as she drew near to the Mohaka River
bridge she became filled with apprehension because,
now that she came to think of it, she realised she was
poking her nose into something that did not even
remotely concern her.

When the road dipped down to the curved span of the
bridge she saw the water far below, snaking its way
between the high rock walls of a narrow gorge. A short
time later, on the other side, she came to a noticeboard
set at the corner of a road which left the main highway.
Stopping the car to examine it, she was surprised to
learn that it indicated the way to Wilder's Wilderness,
which offered the New Zealand experiences of horse
trekking, tramping, native bush walks, camping and
white-water rafting.

Lucy felt intrigued. She had never ridden a horse and,
as she had always lived in the city, the opportunity to
wander through native bush had never come her way.
As for white-water rafting, where an inflated craft shot
between boulders and bounced over foaming rapids, the
mere thought was enough to cause an inward quiver of
fear.

And then she realised that Aunt Bertha had made no
mention of these activities. Was it because she hadn't
known about them? Was that the reason she hadn't said
to watch for the noticeboard? But of course there had
been no communication between her aunt and Silas for

three years, therefore she was unlikely to be aware of what went on at this back-blocks property.

The metal road that left the highway twisted between pine-clad hills for more than a mile before it dropped to the lower level of a wide plateau that stretched along the river cliffs. And then the scene changed to one of pasture-lands. There were fences dividing green fields where sheep, cattle and horses grazed, while in the distance were higher fences forming enclosures for deer.

And then a noticeboard similar to the one on the highway caught her attention, and beside it was an entrance to a tree-lined drive. She turned in, then felt her nerves flutter as she drew up before a timber-built single-storeyed house which was backed by several small chalet-type huts, while behind them were numerous sheds.

Inside the main entrance was a counter, and behind it a door led into the office. A woman in her mid-fifties emerged from it and, despite the fact that hazel eyes smiled at her, Lucy thought she looked rather pale, almost as if she were feeling unwell.

A book lying on the counter was opened, and while pushing back auburn hair the woman asked, 'Did you have a reservation?'

'No, I'm afraid not.'

'You've been here before to sample our outdoor entertainments?'

'No, but I've heard about the place, and I must say they sound as if they're rather exciting,' Lucy said with a certain amount of truth. 'Would it be possible to stay here for a few days?'

'Yes, of course. Have you a special interest in any of our activites? At present the river is quite exciting because the spring rains are keeping it high. But if you're a rider who likes a mettlesome horse I'm afraid you'll find ours are fairly quiet. We get so many people who have never ridden before, therefore we dare not put them on anything that is too high-spirited.'

'I think I'd prefer a bush walk,' Lucy said. 'I've never been in New Zealand native forest,' she added wistfully.

'There's an extensive bush area here,' the woman said, 'but you must keep to the tracks. By the way, I'm Stella. I'm the hostess and I take care of the bookings. The chalets are kept for groups, but I can give you a room in the house.'

'Thank you, I'd prefer a room—a single one if possible.'

'If you'll just sign the book I'll take you to one.'

Lucy hesitated for the merest second. Would Silas see her name, recognise it as a connection to Bertha, and then ask her to leave? It was unlikely, because there were numerous Telfords in the phone book, and in any case it was something she'd have to risk.

She wrote her name, then followed Stella to a room that was small, but adequate. It had a wash-basin, but the showers and toilets were nearby in the passage.

Stella said, 'The dining-room is at the end of the passage.' Then, looking at the deep blue trousers and top Lucy wore, she added, 'Nobody changes into anything dressy for dinner. Everyone remains extremely casual, because it's that sort of a place, you understand. Now I'd better check the answering machine. . .'

Left to her own devices, Lucy wondered what she should do next, then realised she had little option but to wait until she ran into Silas. At the same time she couldn't help feeling surprised by the discovery that all was not as Aunt Bertha had surmised. Apparently her aunt had been unaware of the outdoor activities, and instead of being an undeveloped shambles Wilder's Wilderness had an atmosphere of stability.

'It's just an hour's run to the turn-off,' Bertha had assured her. 'You can leave here in the morning, find

Silas and talk to him, then return by evening. There's no need to take your suitcase.'

But Lucy had felt doubtful. 'You make it sound very easy, Aunt,' she'd said. 'But it might not be quite as simple as you imagine. I think it's a matter that should be approached slowly, perhaps making it necessary to stay overnight, or even for a few days. In that case I have my cheque-book to pay for accommodation.'

'I'll reimburse you, of course,' Bertha had assured her. 'But please let me know whether or not you'll be home this evening—otherwise I'll be watching and waiting for you.'

And now that Lucy had resolved to stay for a few days, she decided to tell her aunt to expect her when she saw her. And with this in mind she returned to the reception desk to ask Stella if she could use the phone.

Stella smiled affably. 'Of course—come into the office. I'll unplug the answering machine.' She then remained in the office to continue with the task of checking a list of some sort.

With Stella so close at hand it was necessary to make the conversation with her aunt brief and to the point, although with Bertha this was not always easy. However, Lucy managed to convey that she intended to stay for several days, or perhaps for even a week. Then, as she was about to replace the receiver, a deep male voice came from behind her—a voice she'd heard only recently.

'Well, I'll be damned,' it drawled. 'If it isn't Miss Cornflower, the lady who refused to give me a lift.'

She swung round to stare wordlessly at the driver of the utility truck, who now leaned nonchalantly in the doorway.

He went on, 'You were actually on your way to this place—which almost amounts to insult being added to injury.'

She found her tongue. 'I'm sorry—I didn't know you were coming here——'

'And in any case—you'd promised *Mummy*.' His tone was sardonic.

Stella said, 'You sound as if you've met before.'

The man spoke harshly. 'Indeed, yes—on the main highway. Matt and I ran out of gas, for the simple reason that the dear old boy had forgotten to fill up while I was with the wholesaler. Nor did I notice this fact until we were well on our way home.'

'Did you get everything on the list I gave you?' Stella asked anxiously. 'I hope you didn't forget the barbecue sausages.'

'They're here. We remembered everything except the all-important commodity to get the lot home.'

'He's getting old,' Stella excused kindly.

'Rubbish. He's only in his sixties. Nowadays that's not old.'

'So how did you get home?' Stella queried.

'Fortunately a fellow with a spare can of petrol came along. He agreed to sell it to me.'

Lucy said with a hint of triumph, 'I *told* you another car would come along soon.'

'So you did.' The words came mockingly.

Stella seemed to sense the coolness between them and, perhaps in an effort to ease the tension, she said hastily, 'This is Miss Lucy Telford, Silas. She's just booked in.' Then to Lucy she added, 'This is Silas Wilder. We call him the boss.'

Lucy became conscious of shock. This was Silas Wilder—the man she'd come to see? She then noticed that his eyes had narrowed while surveying her critically, and she heard his next words with apprehension.

'Lucy Telford,' he mused softly. 'Now where have I heard that name? Somehow it rings a bell. Where do you come from, Miss Telford—or do I appear to be inquisitive?'

'Not at all, Mr Wilder. I've written it in the book. I'm from Wellington.' Was he about to realise she was Bertha's niece? she wondered a little nervously.

'You're on holiday, I presume.'

'For only a short time. I heard of this place and felt interested,' she informed him with truth, or at least part truth.

'You heard of this place from as far afield as the capital city? Most satisfactory, I must say.'

Lucy regarded him frankly. 'Do you question all your guests in this manner, Mr Wilder?'

'Only when something niggles at me—something I can't put my finger on,' he admitted cheerfully.

'You're saying that something about me niggles at you?' Lucy demanded with great daring.

'Yes—you could say so. When I discover what it is I'll let you know.' He grinned in a more cheerful manner, then left the office.

Lucy felt slightly bewildered, but hid the fact as she turned to Stella. 'Did you say you call him the boss?'

'Yes—he's been the boss for three years. The person he referred to as Matt is his uncle. He used to own the property, but he didn't seem to have the interest to do anything with it. Until Silas came it was nothing more than a wilderness.'

'He made a difference?' Lucy found difficulty in concealing her interest.

'Did he ever! His father had died and he bought the property with money he'd inherited from the estate. The fences were put in order, the fields were top-dressed with necessary fertilisers, and even Matt took on a new lease of life. Of course, it's the farm that keeps the place going financially. The outdoor adventures are looked upon as fun and relaxation, although I must say they pay their way.'

Despite herself, Lucy heard a question being dragged from her lips. 'Is he married?'

Stella shook her head. 'He is not—nor is he likely to be as far as I can make out—although Matt dropped a hint that there had been someone at one stage. If this is true she hasn't been near the place—at least, not since Bill and I have been here.'

'Bill. . .?'

'My husband. He grows vegetables, helps with the farm, and guides the horse treks. He should be in with a party quite soon.'

Lucy became conscious of sudden guilt. 'I'm hindering you,' she apologised contritely. 'I'll go to my room and freshen up.'

'Dinner is at six-thirty,' Stella informed her. 'I know it's early, but outdoor activities make people ready for a meal.'

When she reached her room Lucy lay on the bed to review the situation, the main point occupying her mind being the fact that Silas was not yet married to Doreen. Her thoughts then returned to part of the conversation with her aunt.

'I blame Doreen for his behaviour,' Bertha had declared. 'Mind you, I don't think he was madly in love with her. I think she'd become a habit with him, if you know what I mean—and of course *she* was at the root of the trouble between Silas and me.'

'In what way, Aunt?' Lucy had queried.

'In the *cruel* manner in which she tried to prise me out of my home.' The memory had caused Bertha to quiver with anger. 'It began after my dear Tom had passed away and when Silas and this woman spoke of becoming engaged. Of course she *knew* that Silas had inherited this property, but what she *hadn't* realised was that I have the right to live in the house for my lifetime, or until I happen to marry again. Needless to say I've no intention of committing myself to *that* particular folly. Oh, no—indeed no——'

'So—what happened?' Lucy had queried.

'Well—Doreen, being *Doreen*, performed. She flew into a rage and vowed she would not accept Silas's ring until he'd evicted that bossy, domineering woman from the house in which they would begin their married life.' Bertha had drawn a deep breath. 'My dear—*she* was referring to *me* as being bossy and domineering. Can you believe it?'

Lucy could, and had been unable to meet her aunt's eye while stifling a strong desire to giggle. In an effort to control her mirth she'd asked, 'What was Silas's reaction?'

Bertha had snorted. 'Naturally, he agreed with Doreen. Would you believe he had the temerity to suggest that this house is too large for one person? He also had the cheek to suggest I should move into a flat nearer town. I told them I had no intention of budging an inch from this place, and if they couldn't be civil they could both keep away. Then I began to lose my temper——'

'With the result that he really did keep away,' Lucy had pointed out. 'So what happened about the engagement?'

'It was definitely off—especially when Doreen refused to live in a flat while he owned this house.'

'It sounds as if she wanted this house more than she wanted him,' Lucy mused, knowing that if she herself loved a man she'd be happy to live in any humble abode.

Now that she had met Silas Wilder, Lucy realised it would not be easy to persuade him to visit his stepmother, and once again she wondered why she had been stupid enough to have allowed herself to become involved in this situation. But now that she was here she supposed she'd better do her best, although obviously it was not a matter to be rushed. Also, before she broached the subject, she'd be wise to become more friendly with Silas, because antagonism would get her nowhere.

A quick glance at her watch showed that she would

have time for a short walk outside before dinner, and
with this in mind she sprang from the bed and raked a
comb through her hair. Then she stepped out into the
crisp early evening air to find the western sky streaked
with reds and golds, and the shadows in the distant hills
turning to violet.

Turning her back on the sunset, she crossed the yard
to where a track, wide enough to take a vehicle, led
down to the river. She followed its descent to the water's
edge, then looked across to where a high rock wall was
studded with clumps of ferny growth that had found soil
in crevices.

As she stared up at the height a voice spoke from
behind her, and she turned to discover that Silas Wilder
had followed her down the track. The sight of him made
her catch her breath.

'Are you thinking of scaling that wall?' he asked with
a hint of mockery in his voice. 'We don't really encourage
rock climbing among our activities. There's always the
danger of a guest landing in a heap on those boulders.
They might look round and smooth, but they're mighty
hard. As for the cliffs, they're very slippery.'

She recalled her resolve to be friendly, therefore she
laughed as she said, 'You'll have little trouble from me
in that respect. Even if they stretch as far as I can see,'
she added, looking up and then down the river.

'Most of the Mohaka is entrenched in deep gorges,
some of them quite spectacular,' he informed her. 'It's a
fierce river, full of rapids and boulders, plus the odd
small waterfall.'

'Yet it seems to have a song of its own,' she said
whimsically.

He sent her a sharp glance. 'You can hear it?'

'Yes.' She put her head back and closed her eyes. 'If I
shut out everything except the rushing of the water I can
hear different levels of sound.' Then her eyes flashed

open as she said doubtfully, 'I suppose you think it's just my silly imagination.'

'No. I've heard that song. It alters with the state of the river. I mean whether it's high or low, and that means it has a winter song and a summer song.'

Again she looked at him doubtfully. 'Why do I get the feeling you're patronising me?'

'Nothing could be further from the truth, Miss Telford,' he assured her smoothly. 'In fact it was the song of the river that put the idea of white-water rafting into my head. That, and its Maori name.'

'You mean Mohaka? What does it mean?'

'A place to dance—or so it's said. Thinking about it, I saw the rafts dancing over the rapids and through the white foam.'

She said, 'Long ago, Maori canoes would have danced along its length.'

'Are you interested in taking a raft trip, Miss Telford?'

'Not at all, thank you,' she replied firmly.

'Then it was the horse-riding that brought you here?'

She hesitated, wondering if he had already begun to suspect her identity. Then, realising that sooner or later he must be given a reason for her presence, she repeated the one she had given Stella. 'It was the thought of a bush walk that caught my fancy,' she said without actually meeting his eye. 'Is it possible to see native birds? How I'd love to see a kiwi—or even a weka.' She looked at him eagerly. 'Are there kiwis in your bush, Mr Wilder?'

'Yes—a few. But they're nocturnal birds, therefore they are seen only at night. Perhaps it can be arranged.' Glancing at his watch, he added, 'It's time we made our way to the dining-room. Allow me to assist you up the hill.'

Unexpectedly he reached to take her hand, his touch sending a shock of tingles up her arm and through her body. And while she knew she needed no assistance, her own clasp became firmer as his grip became more tense.

They parted at the front entrance, Silas favouring her with a brief nod before striding away. And when she reached her room Lucy told herself her flushed cheeks were merely the result of the climb up the slope. It had nothing to do with the fact that—*that man*—had thought it necessary to almost drag her to the top. However, his attentions had been rather nice, she admitted to herself while taking extra care with her make-up before going to the dining-room.

Stupidly, she had hoped that Silas would invite her to sit at his table, but instead she was led to a small one by a girl she later learned to be Stella's daughter, Jean. From its position near the window she noticed that Silas and an older man occupied a corner table, while a party of sixteen young men was divided between the four central tables.

She also noticed that at times Silas left his table to chat with his guests, and even as she wondered if he'd come to her table he sat in the chair opposite her, his presence making her feel warm.

'Are you enjoying that trout, Miss Telford?' he queried, his eyes on the flush rising to her cheeks. 'It was caught in the river.'

'And cooked by an expert,' she smiled, trying to remain calm.

'I'll pass on your comment to Ling, our chef. He'll be delighted.'

Before anything further could be said, a middle-aged man entered the room and approached Silas. 'Stella won't be in for dinner,' he said in a low voice. 'She says she feels sick and can't eat anything—on top of which her right side is giving her pain. I'm afraid it could be her appendix.'

'Take her to the doctor at once,' Silas said abruptly.

'I suggested it, but she's determined to wait until the morning because she's hoping it'll wear off.'

'If it becomes worse you'll wish you'd put your foot down and that she was in Hastings Hospital,' Silas said. 'By the way, this is Miss Telford—Bill Martin,' he introduced belatedly.

Bill nodded absently to Lucy, but with his mind full of his own problem he said to Silas, 'I know you're right, boss—and you know what women are like——'

'Only too well.' The words came bitterly. 'There's no need to tell me how determined they can be.'

Lucy felt irritated. 'Is there some reason why we shouldn't have minds of our own?' she demanded sharply.

'It depends upon the circumstances,' Silas retorted coolly. 'In this case I'm surprised that Stella hasn't had the sense to allow Bill to take her to a doctor in Hastings right away.'

Bill sprang to his wife's defence. 'It was upsetting the work schedule she'd planned,' he explained, glancing towards the tables where the banter and laughter among the sixteen young men made the lowering of his voice unnecessary. 'Those fellows did their horse trekking today, and tomorrow they're due to go rafting. They're leaving this place in the afternoon and we have another lot coming in, so Stella has arranged for Jean to attend to the chalets and bed changing while she does the barbecue at the end of the rafting.'

Lucy said, 'May I point out that even if she's here I doubt that she'll be well enough? I thought that she looked very pale when I arrived this afternoon. Didn't you notice?' she asked, turning towards Silas.

He looked at her in silence for several moments before he said, 'It's possible my mind was on something else— Miss Cornflower.'

'Like people refusing to give you a lift?' she queried sweetly.

He ignored her words by reverting to the former subject. 'Ling will have to help me with the barbecue. It's served at the end of the raft trip,' he explained to Lucy. 'Ling is Chinese. It'll make a change for him to cook in the open instead of the kitchen.'

'I'm afraid he can't do that, boss,' Bill said. 'There are four women coming for lunch. They're from one of the country Women's Institutes, and they're coming to check out the suitability of the bush walk for a much larger party—most of them elderly. Of course, one of the raft guides could help you,' he added thoughtfully.

'They'll both be showering and changing into dry clothes with the rest of the party,' Silas pointed out curtly. 'I'm not having anyone hanging round in a wet suit for the sake of cooking a sausage.'

Watching him stare gloomily at the table, Lucy said impulsively, 'Perhaps I could help. At home we often have barbecue teas because it's my father's favourite way of entertaining friends or clients. I've barbecued chops and sausages galore.'

'I can't ask you—a guest——' Silas began stiffly.

'You haven't asked me. I've offered,' she pointed out, then added, 'Perhaps it would help to make up for that other time when I refused to help.'

'If you're sure you don't mind—I'd be most grateful,' he said.

'But not more grateful than Stella,' Bill put in. 'I'll go and give her the good news.'

CHAPTER TWO

SILAS said, 'When you've finished your dessert, Jean will serve your coffee at my table. I'd like you to meet my uncle.'

Was it an invitation or an order? she wondered. His authoritative tone seemed to indicate the latter, giving the impression that here was a man who expected to be obeyed.

He went on, 'Matt lived here alone for years before I came on the scene. He had previously managed a South Island high-country sheep station which consisted of thousands of acres, therefore he looked upon this three-thousand acre block as a mere pocket-handkerchief. He's something of a hermit by nature and imagined he could cope with it all by himself, apart from getting in labour when necessary.'

'But he was unable to do so?' Lucy looked across the room to where the older man sat at the corner table. Grey-haired and with a grey moustache beneath his aquiline nose, the man who had peered at her from the utility truck when she had stopped on the highway was not difficult to recognise.

'The first lesson he learnt was that the place needed the strength of a younger man,' Silas explained. 'And with his money tied up in the land he lacked the extra cash necessary to turn it into a paying proposition.'

'You mean he was undercapitalised?' she queried with insight.

'That was it exactly.' He paused, regarding her steadily before he asked, 'You have a job in Wellington, Miss Telford?'

'Yes—I work in my father's office. He's an accountant

with rooms near Oriental Bay, Mr Wilder.' Now why
did she have to blab that piece of information? she
wondered, becoming thoroughly irritated with herself.

However, it did not appear to hold any particular
significance for him because he merely said, 'The name
is Silas, Lucy.' And, having established the fact that
formalities were at an end, he went on, 'Let me tell you
a little about tomorrow. The two rafts will set off down
the river at ten o'clock, each holding eight plus a guide.
Between three and four hours later they'll arrive at a
point about thirty miles from here.'

Her eyes widened. 'Thirty miles! How do they get
home? I can't imagine them pushing all the way back
against the river.'

He laughed. 'Indeed, no. Matt and I will each drive a
Bedford minibus, one hauling a trailer to carry the rafts
and barbecue equipment home. We'll be at a certain
place to meet them.'

'The road goes so far. . .?'

'Yes. It gives access to several farms beyond this one.
At the most distant property there are shearers' quarters
which enable us to have the use of hot showers, and
shelter for the barbecue if it happens to be raining.
Needless to say, we get there long before the rafters
arrive. The barbecue is hot and ready, and the water
has been turned on to heat for their showers. Their wet
suits are dumped on the trailer and they change into
warm clothing which we've brought with us in a
minibus.'

'It sounds like an exciting performance,' she said.

'I can assure you it's very different from life in an
accountant's office,' he informed her drily.

'You know about life in an accountant's office?' she
asked with a degree of innocence, while knowing perfectly well that he did.

'I was in one—before I changed my lifestyle,' he said
abruptly.

She contemplated him in silence, wondering if this new lifestyle was one that completely excluded women— Aunt Bertha and Doreen in particular—but he did not enlighten her. Instead he kept to the present subject.

'Ling prepares the food,' he said. 'It will be carried in a large hamper. Your job will be to place it on the barbecue and keep it turned. You'll find there are more than just sausages.'

'I must admit I'm looking forward to it,' she admitted with truth.

'You are? Good.' The brown eyes regarded her in a contemplative manner until he said, 'You must meet Matt. I should warn you—you'll find he's a rather silent type where women are concerned. Once he was badly let down, and since then he's never looked at another female.' Despite the suggestion, he made no effort to move.

Deliberately, she took him literally. 'Are you saying he shuts his eyes when confronted by a woman, or does he just turn away?'

'He's too polite to do anything quite so blatant. At first I wondered if a little of the South's high-country ice had crept into his blood, but since I've been here he's begun to thaw.'

She regarded him frankly. 'So—does that make two of you?'

His eyes narrowed slightly. 'What do you mean?'

'Were you also sent running to the hills by a woman? Is that why you joined your uncle?' This, she realised, must be her method of approaching the subject of Aunt Bertha. She must encourage *him* to talk about the reason for his desire to change his lifestyle, and to join his uncle in this remote area, rather than try to question him herself.

And the moment he mentioned his stepmother she'd be given the opportunity to tell him how very unhappy Bertha had become. However, she realised that these matters would just have to take their course, although she must also remember she didn't have unlimited time at her disposal, because her father would be expecting her back at the office.

'You've become very silent,' he remarked, breaking into her thoughts. 'What's going on behind those corn-flower-blue eyes?'

She smiled. 'Nothing of importance. Take me to meet your uncle—before he runs away.'

Matthew Wilder rose to his feet as they approached the corner table, and instead of shutting his eyes or turning away he scrutinised Lucy with interest. Silas introduced them, and in an effort to make amends for the earlier incident on the highway she held out her hand and spoke quietly.

'I'm sorry about this afternoon, Mr Wilder. I'm sure you'll understand that a girl can't be too careful.'

'You were quite right,' he said gruffly. 'Secretly I applauded your decision.'

'She's almost on the staff,' Silas put in. He went on to tell his uncle about Stella, and Lucy's willingness to assist with the next day's barbecue for the rafting party.

'Allow me to add my gratitude,' the older man said fervently. 'I'm useless with that contraption. Give me a good electric stove any day, or even an old-fashioned wood range.'

Silas laughed. 'I'll admit you had cause for complaint when we used charcoal that needed a good layer of white ash before we could start cooking. During the day it was difficult to judge when the charcoal was at the correct stage.'

'You can't see the pinkish glow that tells you the fire is ready,' Lucy said in agreement.

'So we now take the easy way out by using gas which we carry with us.' Silas grinned. 'It removes my firing-up frustrations.'

Matt said with satisfaction, 'At least the billy tea is

made in the approved fashion. Have you tasted tea made
with water boiled in a billy hung over a wood fire, Miss
Telford?'

'No, I haven't. And please call me Lucy.'

'It's Matt's speciality, so you have a treat in store.'
Silas grinned. 'At least it's made in the genuine outdoor
manner with the billy of water suspended from an iron
bar over the flames. Matt's even fussy about the wood
he burns.'

'And with good reason,' Matt said with decision. 'Any
fool can tell you that the billy never boils over wood that
is wet. Our native manuka that burns with a hot, clean
flame is best——'

He was interrupted by Bill Martin's return to the
room, his jaw set in a determined line. When he reached
the corner table he spoke to Silas. 'I'm taking Stella to
Hastings right now. I've phoned the doctor, and he's
arranged for her to be admitted to hospital for obser-
vation, or whatever they do. I'll stay there until I know
something definite.' He placed a hand on Lucy's
shoulder. 'She has asked me to express her gratitude to
you, but I don't know how to find the words.'

Lucy smiled at him. 'Please tell her I'm sorry she's
ill—but that I'm pleased to be able to stand in for her.'

'May I tell her you'll fill in until she returns?' Bill
asked anxiously. 'I'm afraid it's very indefinite.'

'If—if Silas wishes me to do so,' she said doubtfully.
'He may have somebody else in mind.' Her thoughts
had leapt to Doreen.

'I have nobody else in mind,' Silas assured her. 'But
you must realise that Stella could be away for quite a
period—especially if her appendix is to be removed.'

She looked at him reflectively, realising it would give
her more time to cope with the task that concerned him.
However, all she said was, 'I'll have to phone my father.'

'Will he demand your return?' Silas asked.

She shook her head. 'It's unlikely. He knows I have

extra time off owing to me because my last holiday period was cut short when one of the staff became ill. I'll ask if I can arrange to take it now. I'm sure he'll agree.'

'You can tell him you've slipped on to my payroll,' Silas said.

She laughed. 'Oh, no—I can't see that payment will be necessary. I'll be thoroughly enjoying myself.'

Silas remained serious. 'I thought you'd agreed to take Stella's place. She also acts as my hostess. She attends to the reservations, and when people arrive she shows them to the chalets she's arranged for them to occupy.'

Matt put in, 'Departing guests pay their accounts at the office, where she gives them a receipt, and Ling takes his list of commodities to her—things to be ordered for the kitchen, you understand.'

Silas went on, 'You must also realise that standing in for Stella has more to it than turning a sausage on the barbecue. That's really just a little relaxation to give her a break from the office job.' He paused, looking at her thoughtfully. 'Perhaps you haven't been given the opportunity for sufficient consideration. Is it possible the job is too difficult for you? It's very different from facing a computer all day.'

'It sounds much more interesting,' she said.

Matt looked at her from beneath grey, shaggy brows. 'You mustn't forget the answering machine. It has to be checked for any messages that could've been left.'

Silas regarded her with a hint of mockery. 'Am I right in suspecting you feel you've bitten off more than you can chew?'

Her brows rose as she bristled inwardly. 'You mean more than I can cope with? You're suggesting that these simple tasks are beyond my capabilities?'

He frowned. 'Not exactly. But I am wondering if they are tasks that have no appeal to you because they're completely lacking in glamour.'

'What makes you imagine I need glamour?' she queried. And then enlightenment dawned as the thought of Doreen flashed into her mind—Doreen who had insisted upon living in the pretentious home, rather than in a humble flat. 'Have you been associated with someone who demands glamour?' she asked innocently, then immediately regretted the question.

His mouth tightened. 'What makes you think that could be the case?' he rasped irritably.

She smiled. 'Are you admitting I've hit the nail on the head?'

He scowled at her, but said nothing.

She went on, 'This woman—whoever she is—are you judging all others by her?'

Matt gave a snort of amusement. 'Good question—but don't bother to deny it, laddie. Lucy will soon learn that you're not exactly a ladies' man. Now why don't you introduce her to the office routine—and perhaps show her the chalets?'

'But it's dark,' Lucy protested.

'Well—I thought that as the moon is almost full——' Matt began.

'Thank you—I'd prefer to see them in full sunlight,' Lucy said hastily, in case Silas imagined she was anxious to experience a moonlight stroll with him.

'Quite right,' Silas said gruffly, while directing a cool glare towards his uncle.

The older man stood up. 'Well—if you'll excuse me I'll go to my room, where I have a good book. You can at least show Lucy the office, Silas. She needs to phone her father.'

A few minutes later Silas led Lucy into the office, where he checked the telephone's anwering device for messages, then, having unhooked it from the phone, he said, 'There you are—it's all yours.'

'Thank you.' She then hesitated, waiting for him to leave the office so that she could speak to her father in private, but he made no move to do so. Instead he examined the book containing future reservations, then began to study a pile of accounts. Nor did she dare ask for privacy, because to do so would look as if she had something to hide—which in fact she did.

Sighing a little, she gave a mental shrug and lifted the receiver. Moments later her father answered the call, his voice coming as clearly as if he were in the same room, and even loudly enough for Silas to hear it.

And with Silas listening to both sides of the conversation it was impossible to explain the situation thoroughly, therefore she said, 'Daddy—it's Lucy—I'm at a place called Wilder's Wilderness—you reach it by turning off the Taupo road.'

'Really?' His voice held surprise. 'I thought your mother said you were going to——'

She cut in over his words. 'Oh, yes, but I've been there. Daddy—you know I have time due to me. Do you mind if I take it now?'

'I suppose it's all the same if I do,' he grumbled.

'I'll tell you all about it when I get home,' she said, hoping he'd caught the urgency in her voice.

There was a silence before he asked, 'How much time do you want?'

'I'd—I'd like a fortnight—*please*, Daddy——'

His voice came grimly. 'If you're away to glory in some sort of wilderness I suppose I haven't much option—but I must say that this is mighty strange——'

'Thank you, Daddy.' Again she cut in over his words. 'Goodbye.' The receiver was replaced before he could demand further details or ask if she wished to speak to her mother—which would be fatal, because Mother would surely mention Bertha's name. She then turned to find Silas watching her. 'Well—that's OK,' she said with a sense of relief.

'I could hear his voice,' he admitted. 'He didn't sound particularly overjoyed.'

'No—but I know they'll manage without me. And when my father gives it a little thought he'll realise it is now September and that my time off is likely to creep into next year, which will make a much longer period owing to me.' She paused, then changed the subject by looking at him expectantly as she said, 'Haven't you things to show me about the running of this office?'

He gave a rueful smile and flicked a handful of papers. 'You mean apart from the cheques to be written out for these accounts? Yes, indeed, there's plenty to show you.'

He placed the accounts on the desk, then drew her towards a map on the wall. 'This will give you an idea of the property,' he said, then, with one hand resting upon her shoulder, he pointed out the farmland area with its manager's house and men's quarters, the main homestead and four chalets, and the bush area adjoining the far end of the three thousand acres.

By that time she had become vitally conscious of the pressure of his hand on her shoulder. For some strange reason it was causing her breath to quicken, which in turn was causing her heart to hammer more rapidly. And even while considering whether or not to remove it gently, she seemed to lack the power to do so.

Telling herself she was an idiot, she pulled her thoughts together and made an effort to concentrate upon what he was saying, and as she listened to the pleasant tones of his deep voice she realised he was on the subject of white-water rafting.

'It takes place only when we can fill two rafts,' he explained, 'otherwise it doesn't pay for itself.'

She thought quickly. 'So that when this activity is called for it must be for a party of sixteen with the four chalets free to accommodate them. You did say four to a chalet?' She looked up and found his eyes resting upon her, an inscrutable expression hidden within their depths.

'That's right. I can see you're catching on quickly. As

for the bush walks, nobody goes there without a guide—
which is something I hope you'll remember.'

'Aren't there tracks?' she queried.

'Yes, there are tracks, but that doesn't mean that
people keep to them. The temptation to follow a fantail
flitting in front of one's face is often hard to resist. And
there are people who leave the track while trying to
gather a few ferns. By the time they've got what they
want the rest of the party has disappeared—and the
track is also out of sight.'

'So what happens?'

'The guide, who has driven them there in a minibus,
naturally counts heads before he starts on the return
journey. If there's one missing he has to make a search.
I can assure you it's very easy to become lost in the New
Zealand bush, and this one stretches over a large area.'

'Then it's not all on your property?'

He laughed. 'Heavens, no. We only intrude into its
edge.'

He took his hand from her shoulder, and she was
startled by the sense of loss caused by its removal.
However, she gave no sign of having been aware of its
presence, and watched with interest while he pointed to
a red line that wandered over the map.

'This is the route for the horse trekking,' he informed
her. 'We have more than thirty horses, although not all
are used at once, of course. It's a matter of having spares
for when any of them go lame, or are needed for work on
the farm. Bill Martin normally takes care of the horse
trekking activities.'

'Apart from attending to reservations, the hostess has
other jobs?'

'Naturally. When enquiries are made she gives information concerning the costs and hours of the different
outdoor adventures. There's a list which will give you
all these details at a glance.'

He opened a drawer of the desk to extract a folder of

papers. Their fingers touched briefly as she took it from him, and Lucy almost snatched her hand away. Vaguely, she became aware that this man was having an effect on her, and she put it down to the fact that she was unaccustomed to associating with such a devastating member of the opposite sex. In comparison, the men she knew were mundane.

Looking at the list, she said a little shakily, 'Thank heavens for this. I doubt that I could do the job without it.'

'Thank heavens you're willing to try,' he returned quietly.

Still with her eyes on the list she said, 'I think the place is misnamed. It's too well-organised to be a wilderness.'

He laughed. 'Ah—that's part of my cunning. When I took it over from Matt I realised that a wilderness was something different from the average person's orderly life. And you'll find that this outback area is a far cry from the city's concrete jungle—and therein lies the reason for its charm.'

'I see. So while it's a wilderness on the outside, it's highly controlled below the surface,' she said thoughtfully.

'That's it exactly.' He looked round the office with satisfaction, then said, 'Incidentally, if people arrive after dark, this extra switch lights the way to the chalets.'

'You appear to have thought of everything.'

He shrugged. 'I suppose it's become my life—my number one priority.'

She looked at him wordlessly while wondering how to express the questions seething about in her mind, and at last she gathered sufficient courage to ask, 'Are there no women in your life, Silas?'

His mouth twisted into an angry line as he snarled, 'Women are the last commodity I need in my life.'

'But—don't you realise that nothing is any good

unless it is shared?' It was something her mother had always declared to be a fact, and suddenly Lucy saw the truth of it.

'I do share it—with Matt,' he declared stubbornly. 'I've relieved him of the financial burden, but we both share the interest of the place.'

'Matt won't always be with you,' she pointed out quietly. 'When he goes there'll be just you—alone in your wilderness. Think about it.'

'Perhaps. . . Some day I'll give it thought, but in the meantime I'm far too busy—what with accounts to do in the evenings.'

She contemplated him in silence. Was this a hint that he'd had enough of her company for tonight? Coolly, she said, 'OK—I'll leave you to get on with whatever work will take you to the middle of the night.'

His face showed pained surprise. 'Did I say I wished to end this evening?'

She decided to be frank. 'I imagined I heard a hint of dismissal in your words—so I've decided to go to bed.'

'Very well—as you wish.' The words came in a curt manner.

He'd made no attempt to detain her, she noticed while feeling slightly irritated as she walked along the passage towards her room, but at least she'd indicated she was not falling over herself to bask in the pleasure of his company. So what was this vague sense of excitement that seemed to be stirring within her? Surely it was merely suspense at the thought of the approaching task to be faced on account of Aunt Bertha—or was it apprehension? Yes, that was it—*apprehension*—because the moment Silas realised her true reason for being there he'd turn on the ice and send her to pack her suitcase.

Next morning the sky was blue, although the air was chilly from the frost that covered the ground. Lucy stepped into her warmest black and white trousers and high-necked top, and when the appetising aroma of sizzling bacon and eggs drew her towards breakfast she found the dining-room to be nicely heated by the logs blazing in the large open fireplace. The rafting party was already seated.

She made her way towards the small window table selected for her the previous evening, but before she could sit down Silas came to her side. Her heart gave a sudden lurch as she looked up into his handsome face, and despite herself she sent him a radiant smile.

He appeared to examine her features one by one before he spoke. 'How about bringing it to my table?' he suggested at last.

She felt nonplussed. 'Bringing—what?'

'That lovely smile. It'll brighten the corner. Bill and Stella usually sit with us, and as you're taking her place——'

'It would give us the opportunity to iron out problems?' She spoke slowly while controlling her eagerness to spring to her feet, and as she walked across the room beside Silas one of the rafting party gave a low whistle which was obviously directed at her.

She stood still, then turned and approached the table. 'Good morning, gentlemen,' she said affably. 'I'm the acting hostess. Is everything to your satisfaction?'

There was a silence before one of them said, 'No, it isn't. I'd like you to sit on my knee. I haven't had a pretty girl on my knee for at least a week.'

Lucy smiled at him. 'Then you'd better hurry back to find her. Remember that absence makes the heart grow fonder—of the knee next door.' The remark was greeted with laughter.

When she reached the corner table Silas said with approval. 'Good girl—I can see you'll not be intimidated by some of the cheeky young devils we get here.'

Matt, who was enjoying a plate of porridge, sent Silas a searching glance. 'What makes you imagine that's the first wolf-whistle Lucy has handled? With her face she'll be an old hand at it.'

Silas said nothing, and the subject was dropped.

Later, she stood on the riverbank to watch the launching of the yellow and black rubber rafts. It was a vibrant scene, she thought, the men in bright red wet suits, life jackets and white helmets making splashes of colour against the darkness of the water, which flowed without the hindrance of boulders at this particular area.

She listened while Silas gave them a talk on safety measures, reminding them that if anyone fell out he must lie on his back. He also emphasised the fact that the guide in each raft was the undisputed boss. She watched him check to make sure each man wore a woollen jersey under his wet suit, plus woollen socks and rubber-soled trainers on his feet.

As the men moved to take their seats on the sides of the rafts, each one was handed a paddle. The guide took his place at centre stern and, after the raft had turned in a circle to adjust itself to the current, the paddling rhythm set in to send it down-river towards the white foam that could be seen rising between the distant boulders.

Silas stood watching the rafts until they disappeared round the bend of the Mohaka, then he held out a hand to Lucy. She took it automatically, and together they walked up the hill, neither speaking a word, the only sound in their ears being the song of the river.

When they reached the top his firm clasp loosened, then he dropped her hand to go to Matt, who was loading barbecue equipment on to a trailer attached to the rear of a minibus. Lucy followed to discover that food hampers were already in place, and that there were labelled zipper bags which, she guessed, contained warm clothes for the rafters to change into after their hot showers.

Silas spoke to his uncle, then returned to her side.

'We'll take off before Matt,' he said. 'When you're ready, get into the other minibus.'

She glanced at her watch, then expressed surprise. 'Isn't it too early? I thought you said they'd take about four hours.'

'Yes—but I have something to do on the way. Your anorak looks warm enough, but are you wearing suitable shoes?' He looked down at the jogger casuals she wore, then nodded approval.

A short time later they were making their way along the road that led beyond the property, and had not travelled far before Siles turned the minibus along a side-road that led towards the boundary.

She sent him a rapid glance. 'Where are we going?'

'To the bush. Isn't that why you came here—to experience a bush walk? I wouldn't like you to spend your entire time here without having done so, so I thought a short wander beneath the trees before we join Matt at the landing place would be in order.'

She looked at him gratefully. 'Thank you—you're very kind.'

'Not at all. It's the least I can do for one who has come for a bush walk and then finds the project nipped in the bud by her own willingness to help.'

She bit her lip, feeling a hypocrite. She had not come for the sake of experiencing a bush walk—and her willingness to help had been to gain time to carry out her plan, or rather, Aunt Bertha's plan. And while she longed to tell him the truth, she dared not do so.

How could she have been so pliable in her aunt's hands? Yet if she hadn't agreed to carry out those imperious commands she wouldn't have met Silas—and she knew she was very happy to have met Silas. And then, unexpectedly, she was assailed by the strangest feeling that a greater force than Aunt Bertha had sent her to this place.

His voice broke into her thoughts. 'There it is—the bush—trees that have been standing for hundreds of years.'

The caress in his voice made her turn to him. 'I believe you love it.'

'I believe I do,' he admitted.

They approached what appeared to be a massive green wall, where the sun highlighted tall trunks and sent blue shadows among the tree-tops that seemed to stretch into infinity. In keeping with the rest of the terrain, the land formed hills and valleys, and as she gazed at a hillside Lucy thought that never before had she seen so many different shades of green.

Silas parked the minibus near a gap where a path led into the gloom, and as they trod the leaf-mould their steps made no sound. Nor had they gone far before she was forced to stand still and stare up at tall tree-ferns, their gracefully curving fronds sheltering the path like a row of lofty umbrellas.

Beyond them were towering trees, their branches hung with vines and creepers, their feet hidden by an under-growth of ferns and shrubs. And through it all were shafts of golden splendour, shooting down from above to burnish the leaves with brilliance.

'It's like being in a cathedral,' she said in a hushed voice. 'Have you ever seen the sun's rays streaking through a stained glass window?' She laughed shakily. 'Why am I whispering?'

'Because that's the effect this place has on people—at least on *some* people.' They walked in silence for a short distance before he asked casually, 'You're not gripped by a mad urge to rip up a few ferns?'

Shocked by the suggestion, she stood still to stare at him. '*Rip up*? What are you talking about?' she demanded indignantly.

'It seems to be the ambition of so many women who

come into the bush. They *must* take ferns home to their gardens——'

'Where they die unless the conditions are suitable,' Lucy said. 'My mother is a keen gardener, but she would consider it cruel to lift these ferns from their sheltered positions and subject them to Wellington winds.'

He made no reply, and she wondered if he believed her. Here was a man with little faith in women, she realised. Possibly he'd reached the stage of being one who would merely use them for his own ends—especially his sex life.

They continued along the track, her eyes moving from ferns growing on moss-covered tree trunks to parasites thriving in the twisted tangle of overhead branches. Then, as they turned a bend, Silas unexpectedly stepped closer to her side. A gasp escaped her as his arms clasped her against him, one hand holding her head to his shoulder. If he thinks he's going to kiss me—he's got another think coming, she decided firmly.

He spoke quietly and in a low voice from above her head. 'Keep still. Don't move at all. You said you wanted to see a weka. Look along the path and you'll see one. It belongs to the rail family and is commonly known as a woodhen. Its call is a shrill whistle.'

She relaxed, then became aware of disappointment from the knowledge that he had not had the slightest intention of kissing her after all. She drew a deep breath, and with her cheek pressed against his green woollen jersey she stared at the flightless bird searching for tasty morsels on the path ahead of them.

'It's reddish brown—with strong red legs,' she remarked, feeling conscious of the arms still holding her. 'I've heard they like bright objects. Is that true?'

'Quite true. They're cheeky enough to approach a picnic party for scraps of food, then snatch a teaspoon and make off with it.'

She laughed, then knew she must make a move to

release herself from his embrace—otherwise he'd imagine she was actually *waiting* to be kissed. And as they continued along the path the weka merely stalked into the undergrowth, its short black tail giving a slight twitch as it pecked at whatever caught its reddish eye.

Yet in some strange way the bird seemed to have affected the easy relationship that had previously existed between them and, in trying to analyse her own feelings, Lucy knew that she now felt shy and rather embarrassed.

A quick peep at Silas showed that he scowled as if displeased about something. Was it his own action of having held her against him? Had his anti-female attitude been weakened during an unguarded moment?

As for herself—she had enjoyed the feel of his arms about her. It had been much more exciting than seeing a weka for the first time.

CHAPTER THREE

SILAS's scowl remained on his face as they continued to walk along the track. Lucy noticed he'd quickened his steps, and she found herself almost running to keep up with him.

At last she said a little breathlessly, 'Is anything wrong?'

He stopped and turned to face her. 'What would make you think so?'

'The fact that you're frowning. I wondered if you're angry about—anything in particular. . .'

His brows rose. 'Like what?'

'Like—like forgetting yourself to the extent of putting your arms around me. You appear to be almost running away from the—the dastardly spot where it happened.'

His mouth gave a slight twitch. 'You're the one who should be indignant about that incident.'

'Well, I'm not. I've forgotten it happened,' she lied, 'so you can forget about it also.'

'I've already done so,' he informed her coolly.

The words needled her. 'Then why are you still frowning?' she demanded crossly.

'Actually, I was thinking about the bridge—today's bush walkers, and the fact that the river's up.'

She looked at him blankly. 'To me—a stranger— that's about as clear as mud. Where is this bridge?'

'To be honest it's not a proper bridge, although sooner or later I intend to build one. At present it's merely a few planks covering a narrow part of a stream further along this track.'

'Is it safe?' she asked doubtfully.

'It is when the planks are firmly in place, but they

have to be checked. There's a handrail, but that's of little use if the boards have become dislodged, and that sometimes happens if the stream has been flooded.'

'What happens if a party reaches the bridge and they're unable to cross it?' she asked.

'The guide takes them along other tracks. I'm sure you've noticed there are several branching off on either side. They wander about like a maze. Without a guide you can follow them for hours without finding your way out of the bush.'

The path they were on continued to twist and wind until suddenly he paused to place a hand on her arm. 'Can you hear it?' he asked, his frown returning to mar the handsome features.

She stood still, then nodded as the unmistakable sound of rushing water came to her ears.

'I guessed it would be high,' he said gloomily.

'Sounds like it,' she mumbled, realising that he could hold her in his arms, yet be unaware of her presence because his mind was full of the stream and the bridge. *Charming* she thought, feeling acutely humiliated, especially as it drove home the fact that she'd made little or no impact upon this man.

When they reached the stream they found it to be a rushing torrent that swept in mad haste along a narrow bed. On the far side the force of the high water had separated the outside board from the one next to it, and, crossing the bridge with a few long strides, Silas kicked it back into place.

'Not much trouble here——' he began then shouted at Lucy, '*Get back from the edge!*'

But she had already felt the tremor of unstable ground beneath her feet and, throwing herself back from the danger zone, she was in time to prevent herself falling into the stream. A cry escaped her as her face became scratched by the sharp ends of broken fern fronds, and the next instant she felt Silas lifting her from the damp ground.

He held her against him, nursing her as though she had been a small child, while looking down into her face. 'You've got a few scratches—but I doubt that there are any splinters,' he remarked. 'Do you feel OK?'

She nodded wordlessly, while staring up at him like a hypnotised rabbit. And while she knew she should request to be put down, she was enjoying the feel of being held too much to utter the words. The sting in her face had vanished as though wiped away with a magic cloth, and—*stupidly*—she found herself waiting to be kissed.

But it did not happen. Instead he put her feet to the ground, then took a clean handkerchief to dab gently at the broken skin, saying as he did so, 'There's a first-aid kit in the minibus. I'll give it a touch of hydrogen peroxide.'

'Will it sting?' she asked almost querulously.

'Not as much as it would if real trouble set in,' he retorted drily, then brushed the subject of her wounds aside by glancing at his watch. 'It's time we were on our way. I don't want Matt to struggle alone with the barbecue—and that's precisely what he'll do if I'm not there.'

He's thoughtful for Matt, she realised while hastening to keep up with his long strides, and as they left the shadow of the bush she said, 'I feel as if I'm stepping out of one world and into another.'

'That's exactly what you are doing,' he said. 'This is our world, but in there belongs to the birds. If you go in there and stay perfectly still you'll see numerous varieties—and if you can make it before daylight you'll be almost deafened by a dawn chorus. Now, then—where's that first-aid kit. . .?'

He entered the minibus, then emerged with a white tin that had a red cross on the lid. A swab was soaked

with the antiseptic liquid, and Lucy felt her cheek being
wiped with the utmost gentleness.

'Does it sting?' he asked anxiously.

'A little,' she admitted, and because she guessed he
was waiting for her to flinch she became determined to
show no sign of pain. Instead she stood with her eyes
closed, lest they betrayed the fact that she found him to
be disturbing to her.

The swab moved across her forehead, its touch no
more than a gentle brush, and suddenly she realised
there was no prick attached to it. But even as she
thought about its different feel of smooth dryness instead
of stinging dampness, she suspected she had not felt a
swab on her brow at all. It had been the touch of his
lips.

Her eyes fluttered open, only to find him screwing the
cap to the bottle. Had he kissed her forehead? she
wondered, feeling slightly bewildered. Was there a secret
smile hovering about his mouth? No—it was definitely
her imagination.

A short time later the minibus was making its way
along a metal road that was sorely in need of attention
from a grader. Silas appeared to know every pot-hole,
dip and sharp corner, and was adept in the art of
dodging round them. They passed a few farms, and
Lucy tried to control her nervousness by gazing at the
lonely homesteads, but in some strange way it conveyed
itself to Silas.

'Scared?' he asked casually on one occasion when
going down a steep hill that had a sheer drop on one
side.

Her hair was almost standing on end, but not for the
world would she admit it. 'Should I be—with you at the
wheel?' she queried sweetly.

He grinned. 'I'll bet you've got both feet on the brake.'

She laughed. 'Yes—actually, I have. They're almost

going through the floor, but it's not making the slightest difference.'

'Don't worry—I'll get you there in one piece,' he assured her nonchalantly. 'You're needed for the barbecue.'

The remark was enough to tell her that he *had* kissed her brow, and that he was firmly hauling himself back into the anti-female attitude which would give him security from involvement with a woman.

When they reached the shearers' quarters belonging to the last farm on the road they found Matt drinking tea while he awaited their arrival. He looked with concern at the scratches on Lucy's face, then poured tea which he insisted she drank at once. It was refreshing, and did much to calm her shaken nerves.

Silas and Matt then set up the barbecue, and Lucy was able to open the two food hampers, her eyes widening at the variety they contained.

Silas came to her side. 'There's enough—do you think?'

'Enough! You're certainly generous.'

'They'll be starving. Do you think you can cope with what Ling has prepared?'

She considered the contents to assure herself there was nothing with which she was unfamiliar. Apart from the inevitable sausages, there were numerous chicken pieces, lamb chops and cubed steak on skewers. There were bowls of coleslaw and potato salad laced with green peas, buttered garlic rolls and hard-boiled eggs. She peeped into a foil-covered delicacy to discover split bananas filled with chocolate and walnuts for dessert.

'Does the sight of it frighten you?' Silas asked quietly.

She knew he'd been studying her face while watching for her reaction. 'Oh, no,' she returned calmly. 'Mother and I cook all these things on our barbecue. It was just the thought of coping with this quantity alone that had me momentarily rattled,' she admitted with truth, then added with a hint of defiance, 'But if Stella can do it, I can do it.'

He frowned at her, his irritation suddenly obvious. 'What makes you imagine you've been asked to cope with it alone?' he demanded coldly. 'You must think I'm an inconsiderate devil if you're expecting to be thrown in at the deep end to struggle as best you can.'

'I—I presumed that that was what you intended——'

'Then you're wrong. I'll be with you, watching the food and also serving it. In any case, I don't know how capable you are behind the embers or whatever. Oh, yes—you said that you and Mummy entertain Daddy's guests—but I have yet to learn how good you are at turning out perfectly cooked food. I've no wish to see the hungry rafters sitting down to plates of burnt offerings. It would give the place a bad name.'

Her chin rose as she seethed with anger. 'If you'd prefer to not risk my efforts at the barbecue I can easily set off for home right now. It'll be a long walk, but I'll get there—all in one piece.'

'Are you hinting I'm a reckless driver?' he snarled.

'One of the most reckless I've ever driven with,' she retorted vehemently.

'Thank you,' he gritted, then strode towards the water's edge where he stood staring across the river.

Matt, who had listened to the exchange, laughed. 'Now you *have* touched him on the raw. No man likes to have his driving criticised.' He paused, then laid a hand on her shoulder. 'My dear—don't allow his obsession for everything being first class at the Wilderness get under your skin. I warned you he's not a ladies' man.'

'I'm not sure that he's even a gentleman,' she snapped furiously. 'I wouldn't have offered to help if I hadn't had the experience necessary. Gosh—when I think of the meals I've cooked——'

'But you must admit he hasn't seen your ability, and

you know what men are like. We have to see to believe.'
Matt's tone was full of apology. 'Please don't take it too
much to heart, and for heaven's sake don't cut your visit
short because of it.'

She sent him a reproachful look. 'Didn't I say I'd fill
in for Stella? Haven't I arranged with my father to have
the time off? What makes you think I'll break my word?'

He shrugged, then muttered, 'Only the fact that I've
known women to break their word.'

'Well, you don't know this woman, and neither does
Silas. Nor do I think he had the right to frighten me
while driving here. He went like—like——'

'Like a dog with its tail on fire?' Matt suggested.

'Exactly.' She looked accusingly at Silas, who had
returned from the water's edge in time to hear this part
of their conversation.

'Rubbish,' the latter denied. 'I drove in my usual
manner.'

'Your usual manner, huh?' Matt remarked drily. 'No
wonder the lassie's shirt flew up her back.'

'I had the strangest feeling you were running away
from something,' she said, looking directly at Silas. Then
she added hastily, 'I'd better make a start on fixing the
table.'

She moved quickly to examine the long narrow table
that had forms on either side, and although it looked
clean enough she was not happy until she had washed
it. She waited until it was almost dry before laying a
white plastic cloth along its top, and then plates, cutlery
and bright red paper napkins, found in cartons on the
trailer, were put in place.

She then turned her attention to the food that needed
to be cooked, placing it within easy reach of the barbecue, and making sure the necessary utensils for handling
it were nearby. Nor was she unaware of the interest
Matt and Silas took in her movements, having caught
glances passing between them as they paused to watch

her fold the table napkins round the knives and forks which were left in readiness to be picked up from the end of the table.

The stacks of plates were put beside them, and the bowls of coleslaw, potato salad and other food that did not need cooking were set in place. Yet the table still looked bare, and suddenly she knew it needed flowers. If only she had flowers. . .

Her eyes fell on two empty jam jars standing on a shelf, and then her mind flew to the clumps of snowdrops she'd noticed blooming near the entrance to the shearers' quarters. She hurried outside and hastily picked a bunch of them, and within a short time they were making a pleasing addition to the table.

Matt's reaction to the flowers was enthusiastic. 'Ah— the feminine touch,' he exclaimed with approval.

But Silas was more guarded with his comment. 'We don't normally bother about flowers on the table,' he muttered. 'The men can't eat them, and they can be a nuisance.'

'Even men like the table to look attractive,' she pointed out, disappointed by his response to her efforts.

'I'm sure they'll be impressed,' he retorted drily.

A horrible thought struck her. Did he imagine she'd made a special attempt to impress *him*? 'I can remove them if you find them objectionable,' she said sharply.

'No—don't do that. Actually, I find snowdrops rather insipid,' he admitted as though searching for an excuse for his negative attitude.

She smiled at him. 'Don't you know they stand for hope?'

'Now where would you get that idea?' he drawled.

'From an old fable. On the other side of the world they're called the fair maids of February, but on this side they're known as the sweet maids of September. After a long, cold winter they're a symbol of hope for the new season.'

'So what was this fable?' he demanded with a hint of amusement.

A small laugh escaped her. 'It's really a fairy story that tells of the love between a young prince named Albion, and Kenna, the lovely daughter of Oberon, king of the fairies. But Oberon would not permit the match and drove Albion out of fairyland.'

'The heavy father, eh? Did Albion retaliate?'

'I'm afraid so. He returned with an army, but was slain. Kenna—full of hope—tried to bring him back to life by applying the magic wild herb known as moly, but the moment the juice touched the body it was turned into a snowdrop.'

'So much for her hopes,' he grinned. 'It seems to me that snowdrops speak more of hopelessness than of hope. I told you they're anaemic. And don't forget that "he who lives on hope dies fasting".'

'Are you saying you never hope?' Lucy asked incredulously.

His shoulders lifted in a vague shrug. 'There was a time when I had high hopes,' he admitted. 'But not any more——'

'What did you hope for?' she prompted, then held her breath. Was the subject of Doreen about to come up?

His expression became wry. 'I can't imagine you being even remotely interested in any daydreams I've had in the past,' he said with a slight twist to his mouth.

She caught the bitterness in his tone. Had he been hoping for Doreen to arrive and say she was no longer interested in the large Hastings home and that she'd be willing to live anywhere with him—even to work beside him out in the wilderness?

However, now was not the time to probe into his previous daydreams, and before anything further could be said a shout came from Matt, who had left them to attend to the fire burning beneath the two billies of water which hung from an iron bar. 'They're here,' he called. 'The rafts are being pushed from the river.'

After that there was action. Food was placed to sizzle on the barbecue, and was turned with the help of long utensils, and as she worked beside Silas, moving rapidly to turn first one piece and then another, Lucy became conscious of a feeling of quiet satisfaction.

'I can see you've done this before,' he applauded.

'Didn't I tell you so?' she returned, trying not to sound smug.

The rafters, weary and hungry after their hours of fighting the turbulent Mohaka by paddling their way between rocks and river boulders, spent little time beneath the hot showers and in changing into warm, dry clothes. They were each offered a can of cold beer from a coolbox, and within a short time they were lining up at the barbecue, a plate in hand. Their voices and laughter then filled the shearers' quarters as the two raft parties held a post-mortem on the trip while they ate.

Later came the task of packing the barbecue and hampers on to the trailer which also carried the rafts, and while Silas and Matt stored smaller items away the two raft guides used pails and mops to wash over the floor with hot water. Care was taken to stamp out the fire, and as Lucy watched Silas at work she was struck by his meticulous attention to detail.

Her only task in the clean-up was to empty the two jam jars of snowdrops, but instead of disposing of the flowers she took them with her. Driving home in the minibus, she offered Silas an apologetic smile as she admitted, 'I hadn't the heart to throw them out.'

He stared straight ahead. 'Are you *hoping* for something special?'

She was, but how could she say so? How could she admit she was hoping for the opportunity to have an amicable discussion which would result in his agreement to visit his stepmother? However, she knew that an answer was expected of her, so she said, 'Of course I have hopes. Life would be dull without them.'

He lowered his voice so that it was drowned by the raucous chatter of the men in the rear seats. 'Is it possible you're hoping your boyfriend will follow you here?'

She sent him an enigmatic smile. 'You're not very good at guessing, Silas.'

'But you do have a boyfriend?' he pursued.

'Oh, yes—several. Not that it is your concern.' Then she changed the subject by asking sweetly, 'What are my duties when we reach home? Would you like me to check the mail—or attend to the women who were to go for a bush walk?'

'Both, thank you. You're catching on quite smartly.' He glanced at his watch. 'I doubt they'll be back yet.'

In this surmise he proved to be correct, so Lucy hurried to her room, where she changed her clothes and attended to her make-up. A jar was found for the snowdrops, then she made her way to the office, where she opened a bag of mail and sorted what were obviously accounts, from private letters. Among the latter was a letter for Silas, and as she lifted it she caught the faintest hint of perfume. Could it be from Doreen? she wondered, staring at the mauve envelope.

Even as she pondered the question, Silas came into the office. He glanced through the mail and stuffed the one addressed to him into his pocket without comment.

'It has a lovely perfume,' Lucy said, unable to resist the remark. 'It must be from someone—special.'

'Sniffing at my mail is not part of your duties,' he snapped crossly, then left the office.

So. . .he's in a mighty big hurry to read it, she decided, then wondered why the thought filled her with irritation. But before she could dwell on it a vehicle pulled up at the office door.

Four middle-aged women got out of it, and she

guessed they were the Women's Institute members who had been checking the bush walk on behalf of the Institute. 'How did you enjoy it?' she queried, greeting them with a bright smile.

They bubbled with enthusiasm, all talking at the same time while raving on about the beauty of the bush walk. It was so *different*—the silence was so serene—so *tranquil*—and the birds came so close—and never had they seen such magnificent trees. As for the *ferns*—and here they fell silent as though touched by guilt.

It was enough to make Lucy suspect there were tiny uprooted plants in their handbags, but she said nothing while taking details of their request for lunch and a bush walk on the first Wednesday of the following month.

'There'll be a bus load, which means about forty of us,' one of the women said in happy anticipation.

Lucy felt a sudden qualm. Could they cope with forty for lunch? If only Silas had been there she could have consulted him, but although she looked along the corridor and outside there was no sign of him. However, she checked the guest register to make sure the day in question was not overloaded with outdoor activities, and in fact it was quite free.

It was only after the women had left that she thought to check the receipt book to make sure it had not been her duty to collect payment for today's four lunches, then sighed with relief when she saw that this had been attended to at lunchtime by Jean. Flicking through the register, she then noticed that most of the Wednesdays appeared to have been kept free, and as she pondered this strange fact Silas returned to the office. The scowl on his face indicated displeasure, and after a moment's silence she asked, 'Is anything the matter?'

'Nothing I can't handle,' he returned abruptly, then irriation broke loose as he demanded, 'Tell me, Lucy—what gives women the right to assume so much?'

'Assume? Like what——?'

'Like imagining they can take up where they left off,' he gritted.

'Somebody is doing that?' she queried innocently, her mind darting to the perfumed letter he had received.

'It would appear to be so,' he growled in an undertone, then changed the subject before it could be discussed further. 'I've just spoken to Ted, who took those women into the bush. Normally he's in charge of the deer, but all the staff double as guides. He said they appeared to be happy with their sojourn into the wilds.'

'Very happy indeed. They went out of the door chatting about having seen the land as the early settlers found it. They're coming back on the first Wednesday of next month with a bus load of about forty Women's Institute members——' She broke off as she realised he was staring at her in horror.

'*Forty*—for lunch on a *Wednesday*?' he exclaimed furiously.

Her heart sank. 'Have I done something wrong? I checked and the day seemed to be free,' she quavered. 'Nothing on it at all.'

'Of course it's free,' he snapped. 'Every Wednesday is kept free. It's Ling's day off.'

'But—but Wednesday is their Institute day——'

'I'm afraid they'll have to agree to a change of day, or it'll be cancelled. I'll not have Ling upset. He has his day off in the middle of the week because we are always busy at the weekends. It's his day to visit his mother in Hastings. She's elderly and will be expecting him.'

'I'm sorry—I didn't know,' she whispered.

He ran long fingers through his straight dark hair while exclaiming impatiently, 'It's a pity you couldn't have thought to ask about days off. You must have realised we do have them.'

'It's an even greater pity that *you* couldn't have *told* me about Ling's day off,' she flared at him. 'And it's also a pity you can't be a little more reasonable.

Obviously you're annoyed about that letter you received—but that doesn't give you the right to vent your spleen on me. After all—I'm only the new girl here.'

Distress caused her eyes to brim with tears, and, furious with her own weakness, she turned and went to the inner office window, where she stared through a blur at the tree-sheltered chalets.

He was beside her in a moment, his voice contrite as his hand on her shoulder turned her towards him. Staring down into her face, he said, 'You're right—I'm being unreasonable. It's difficult to remember you're new here—and that you came only yesterday. I don't know why, but I feel I've known you for years.'

She looked up at him in a dazed manner. 'Only yesterday? I seem to have been here for ages.'

'You feel it too?'

She nodded wordlessly, feeling hypnotised by the intensity of the gaze from his brown eyes. They were expressive eyes, she decided, at the moment reminding her of the softness of brown velvet.

'I'm an ungrateful devil,' he murmured. 'Do you forgive me?'

Again she nodded, without speaking.

'Perhaps you'll prove it to this witless fellow who's been so slow to show his appreciation of your willingness to step into the breach caused by Stella's illness.' And without waiting for an answer he drew her closer and lowered his head to find her lips.

The action took her by surprise, and at first she told herself to remain calm and to take the kiss in the spirit it was being given, which was merely a making up between friends after cross words. There was no amorous intent about it, because Matt had assured her that Silas was not a ladies' man. And hadn't Aunt Bertha said he'd gone to join his uncle in this outback place because he was completely finished with women?

So why were his arms tightening about her? she wondered as the kiss deepened. Had his lack of female companionship caused a hunger? And why were her own pulses racing as if the floodgates of her bloodstream had been opened? Perhaps it was because she was unaccustomed to being kissed with such ardour. Kisses she had received—but somehow this was different.

Eventually he released her with what appeared to be reluctance, which was strange, she thought, because she would have expected a man with his inhibitions about women to have just brushed her mouth briefly and then dropped her like a glowing ember. However, the frown on his face did not surprise her, as it probably meant he was annoyed with himself for having been quite so fervent in the way he'd crushed her lips beneath his own.

Leaving her abruptly, he moved to the desk and stood staring down at the papers lying on it, his attitude so tense that Lucy felt compelled to go to his side. She laid a hand on his arm and spoke quietly. 'You're still worrying about Ling.'

He looked at her uncomprehendingly. 'Ling. . .?'

'Yes. I'm sure he'll be able to prepare such things as chicken and ham, coleslaw and other things the day before. It can be on the plates in readiness, and then Jean and I will do the rest. I'm sure he won't mind us going into his kitchen.'

'He's not fanatical about his kitchen.'

'But you're still worried about his day off?'

'I dare say he'll cope with preparing food the day before. He's done it on more than one occasion,' Silas admitted.

She drew a deep breath that betrayed her indignation. 'Is that a fact? Then why were you so mad with me because I made those arrangements?'

'Let it be understood that I was not mad with you,' he said as a bleak expression crept into his eyes.

Her resentment was still bubbling. 'Oh. You could have fooled me.' Then she became calmer as realisation dawned, and she went on accusingly, 'So I was right. It was the letter that really upset you—rather than my stupidity in not being sufficiently clairvoyant to know it was the chef's day off.'

He avoided the issue by saying. 'It's only natural for you to be ignorant about such matters. You know nothing of the running of the place—nor are you likely to be even remotely interested.'

'On the contrary, I am interested,' Lucy found herself admitting. 'Stella said you'd made a huge difference to the place.'

He frowned as though irritated. 'Stella talks too much about my affairs. She's inclined to gossip with complete strangers.'

Lucy sprang to Stella's defence. 'That's only because she thinks all you've achieved is quite amazing. Did you know much about farming before you came here?'

'No—so I brought in experts to handle the work. There's a farm manager and his wife, who have their own cottage, with attached living quarters for two men. You can see peeps of the red roof across the fields beyond the chalets. Bill, Stella and Jean have a flat built on the end of this house, and Ling has his own quarters near the kitchen. All the men, apart from Ling, act as guides in the various adventure activities.'

'It's quite a staff,' she murmured, thinking of the wages to be paid each week, to say nothing of the paperwork.

'The farm pays its own way, and so do each of the outdoor activities,' he said, as though reading her thoughts. 'Farming has seen a recession, but now that more foreign countries are becoming interested in buying our wool there should be an improvement in the wool cheque.' He paused, then said significantly, 'Of course, you'll understand it's a man's world.'

She forced a smile, but it did not reach her eyes. 'You're saying that Stella, Jean and the manager's wife are necessary evils who are merely tolerated for their usefulness? And the same applies to me. My oath—how chauvinistic can you be?' Anger made her voice shake.

He spoke harshly. 'You don't understand the situation——'

Loftily, she cut in, 'I've no wish to do so. It's neither my problem nor my concern.' Then, as she began to think about it, her anger rose, asserting itself to an even greater degree and causing her to almost hiss at him, 'Tell me this—what sort of a hypocrite kisses a woman when he dislikes the entire sex?'

'You exaggerate,' he drawled. 'It's just that I have not yet learnt to trust the species who, as Kipling points out, is more deadly than the male.'

She felt stung. 'It's so *nice* to be considered as being one of a deadly species. Thank you very much.'

'One can only speak from experience,' he retorted.

'*Experience*—as far as *I'm* concerned?' she demanded, aghast.

'No. As far as somebody else is concerned,' he admitted coldly.

'Ah—then somebody *did* send you running to the hills?'

His mouth gave an angry twist. 'You could say so.'

'What did she do?' The question came in a small voice. She had already heard the answer from Aunt Bertha, but here was the out-of-the-blue opportunity to hear it from Silas. At least it would give her the chance to judge his side of the story.

He spoke grimly. 'She pretended she loved me— whereas all she loved were my possessions. A man is not amused by being wanted only for his possessions—or is that too much for the average woman to understand?'

Her chin rose. 'It's a poor, pathetic fellow who imagines all women to be gold-diggers,' she said scathingly. 'Does your own mother come into that category?' She regretted the words the moment they were out.

'My mother died when I was little more than a child,' he informed her quietly. 'However, I have a stepmother.'

'Oh?' Lucy now felt herself to be a hypocrite.

He went on, 'I dare say she's still queen of the Battleaxe Brigade—nor have I any wish to discuss her.'

Lucy bit her lip, then asked timidly, 'That letter you received—I *know* it annoyed you. Why was that?'

He hesitated only briefly before he said, 'Because it asked for a reservation I have no wish to make. However, I suppose it was bound to happen sooner or later. Is the single room next to the one you are in free at the weekend?'

Lucy went to the desk and opened the book. 'Yes—it's free.'

'Then book in Miss Doreen Andrews. . .'

CHAPTER FOUR

DOREEN ANDREWS. Lucy's hand was not quite steady as she wrote the name in the guest register. Without looking at Silas, she asked casually, 'Is this the person who sent you into the outback—the one who has warped your mind against women in general?'

'The same. She's the expert who has shown me how devious the female of the species can be.' His tone had become terse.

'How long is it since you've seen her?'

'About three years. Living out here is inclined to make me lose count of time.'

'Three years,' Lucy mused. 'In that period she could have changed. You might find she's now quite a different person.'

'I doubt it. Does a leopard change its spots?' he queried in a voice that was faintly bored.

She knew he was right. The basic nature of people did not change. They merely became more discerning in the façade they showed to the public. Nevertheless she said, 'Why not give her the benefit of the doubt? Give her the chance to show you that she *has* changed.' Then, looking down at the book again, she went on, 'Are you sure she'll be happy in the room next to mine?'

'It's a suitable room. Why shouldn't she be happy in there?' The question was snapped impatiently.

'Oh, I'm not saying anything against the *room*—it's just that she might prefer the privacy of a chalet——'

'Are you saying there's no privacy in the room next to your own?'

'Well—that's just the point. She'll expect you to visit her and no doubt you'll wish to do so—and—and you'll

both fear that I'll be able to hear through the wall—
whereas in a chalet. . .' She knew she was stumbling
over her words, but at last she said with a rush, 'You
might find yourself falling in love with her all over
again.'

'Is that a fact?' His face had become grim.

'Well—you never can tell,' she said in a weak voice,
then wondered why her thoughts were moving in this
direction.

He eyed her narrowly. 'One would almost imagine
you were trying to push us together. Believe me, I'll be
quite capable of handling the situation.'

More than capable of handling any situation, she
thought, while unobtrusively studying his athletic form
and strong line of jaw. But aloud she merely said, 'I'll
ask Jean to prepare the room for her.' Then, making an
effort to get away from the subject of Doreen, she went
on, 'I haven't checked the answering machine. Would
you like me to?'

He nodded absently, his mind obviously elsewhere—
nor was it difficult to guess in whose direction it had
turned. Nevertheless, the frown still hovered about his
brow, indicating that inner thoughts—or memories—
still raised their heads to nag at him.

Lucy went to the machine, turned back the tape, and
the next instant Bill Martin's voice floated into the office.
He informed them that Stella had not only had her
appendix, but also her gall bladder removed, and that
he would be home in time to attend to the next horse
trek arranged for Saturday. Stella was as comfortable as
could be expected, and hoped Lucy was coping with the
office work. She also said she was sorry that she might
be away a little longer than she had expected to be. Of
course, she sent her love to Jean.

There were no further messages on the tape, and as it
was switched off Lucy found her thoughts being dragged
unwillingly back to the question of Doreen Andrews.

What was she like, this woman who had affected not only Silas, but also Aunt Bertha? In an effort to learn more about her she remarked artlessly, 'Doreen might enjoy the weekend horse trek. That's if she rides, of course.'

'Oh, yes, she rides. She comes from a farming background, but did secretarial courses to enable her to work in the city.'

'Yet she hasn't been out here to see you?'

He spent several moments in thoughtful silence, almost as though wondering whether or not to confide in her. At last he said, 'No. After our break-up she went to Australia for a period. She knew that I was here, and wrote asking what the place was like. I replied, describing the state it was in at that time, and what I hoped to do with it. I had a letter in return to say she'd come when I'd accomplished all I had in mind. She also said she'd like the name changed because she didn't fancy living in a place known as a wilderness.'

'Then—she still expects to marry you?'

'It's one of those situations where marriage between us has always been a foregone conclusion. I've known the family since I was a child. Our parents were friends.'

Lucy looked at him reflectively, now understanding more clearly why Doreen thought she could make demands before a ring was put on her finger. Doreen was one who expected everything, yet gave little in return, she decided. She was not the type of woman necessary for this man's happiness. He could be passionate, she felt sure, and he needed somebody warm and generous with the loving she wrapped about him. Somebody who could meet his own passion. This last thought made her catch her breath.

He noticed the sharp intake. 'Something troubling you?'

'Nothing at all.' Then, raking about in her mind, she said, 'I was merely thinking about the horse trekking. It would be nice to be able to ride. Doreen is very fortunate.'

He looked at her closely. 'Do I detect a wistful note in your voice? How would you like to ride round the sheep with me tomorrow morning? We'd leave after breakfast.'

Her eyes lit as the thought brought a surge of excitement; then her face fell as she said, 'But—I can't ride——'

'You'll not need to ride. All you'll need to do is sit on a horse. I'll saddle Misty for you. She's very quiet. In any case, it's not a cantering or galloping exercise, it's simply a walk among the ewes to make sure there are no lambing troubles or cast sheep.'

'Cast? You mean lying on their backs or sides and can't get to their feet because of their heavy, wet wool?'

'That's right.' His eyes twinkled. 'For a city girl that's very knowledgeable.'

'City girls are not entirely ignorant about country life,' she protested with a hint of indignation.

'But they're inclined to find country life rather dull,' he pointed out.

'Only because the people they love are back in the city,' she reasoned. 'One can be happy anywhere—as long as the right person is near by.'

'Ah—and there lies the problem: to be sure the one near you is the *right* person.' His tone had become thoroughly cynical; then he went on, 'As it happens, I'm more than happy with dear old Matt near by. Actually, he's so like my father it's almost a bonus of having *him* near as well.'

She nodded as she said with sympathy, 'I can understand there must be times when Matt makes you feel your father isn't so far away after all.'

He sent her a glare that was full of suspicion, then demanded abruptly, 'You wouldn't be laughing at me by any chance? I suppose you think I'm an idiot.'

'Of course not. But do tell me—are you saying it

matters what a mere woman thinks of you? No—don't bother to reply to that question. I already know the answer. However, you're most fortunate to be so self-sufficient,' she added drily, while ignoring the darkening scowl on his face.

'There's no need to hide your amusement, Lucy—I'm well aware of it,' he snapped coldly, making no effort to hide his irritation.

'I'll endeavour to keep it under control,' she informed him gravely. 'I'll hold it back until your engagement to Doreen is announced—and then I'll have a loud and hearty laugh.'

'You'll wait a very long time to do that,' he gritted.

She thought carefully for a few moments before she said, 'Silas—aren't you being unreasonable and somewhat unfair to both yourself and to Doreen?'

His brows rose. 'Why do you say that?'

'Because you're not giving yourself a chance to test your own feelings—or to learn whether or not she *has* changed. You're facing the situation with a closed mind.'

'Closed, huh? Then let me assure you the subject of Doreen is also closed.' The words were rasped crossly.

'But Silas——'

'Damnation—must you be so persistent? You are becoming a bore, Miss Cornflower.'

'Stop calling me Miss Cornflower—it's quite stupid,' she hissed furiously. But he was right, she reflected in a burst of mental honesty. She *had* been persistent, and after all it was not her concern. Yet—strangely—it did seem to be her concern, and—equally strangely—she could not decide why it should be so important for her to understand the true state of his feelings towards Doreen.

When Lucy woke next morning a quiver of excitement shot through her, telling her that the day would be different. Of course it'll be different, you ninny, she

reminded herself. You're about to ride a horse. The
thought stimulated her into springing out of bed, showering hastily, and dressing in her warm green trousers
and top. Scant make-up was applied, and her pale gold
hair was treated to little more than a few vigorous
strokes of a brush.

She then hastened to the dining-room, expecting to
find Silas and Matt at the corner table, but there was no
sign of either of them. I'm too late, she thought dismally.
He's gone without me. Farmers are often away at the
crack of dawn. Bitter disappointment caused her to
merely pick at her breakfast until suddenly she was
startled by the sound of his deep voice coming from
behind her.

He carried a pair of jodhpurs. 'See if these will fit
you.'

She looked at the riding trousers, then demanded
bluntly, 'Is it possible they belong to Doreen?'

He sounded bored. 'Good grief—you're refusing to
put them on if they do? You sound very antagonistic
towards her.'

It was true. If they were Doreen's jodhpurs she had
no wish to wear them, so she said, 'I'd prefer to wear my
own trousers.'

'Haven't I told you that Doreen hasn't been here?'

She made no further objection as she held them
against her, instinct telling her that they should fit quite
nicely.

He went on, 'We keep spare articles of clothing here.
There's often somebody who needs the loan of a warm
jacket or anorak. Put them on when you're ready.'

'I'll go and do so at once——'

'You will not. You'll finish your breakfast. I'll not
have the horses frightened by a stomach that rattles
loudly for want of food. In fact I'll have another cup of
coffee.' He sat down and helped himself from the coffee-
pot on the table, then refilled Lucy's cup as well.

Amused, she said, 'Do you treat all your guests in this bossy manner?'

'Only the ones with cornflower-blue eyes. In any case, you're no longer a guest—you're staff.'

'And you're the exacting boss. OK, I'll try to remember it,' she said, conscious of his scrutiny of her face.

A short time later they went out to where a bay gelding and a grey mare were tethered and, after instructing her concerning the correct side to mount, he gave her a leg up.

'It feels so high,' she exclaimed as exhilaration gripped her.

'Don't be nervous,' he advised. 'Horses can sense nervousness in a rider. It gives them the upper hand. Just let her know who is in command.'

'*Command*—huh—that's a laugh,' Lucy quavered.

He mounted the gelding, then turned to smile at her while offering more advice. 'Head up, hands and heels down, elbows in, and grip with your knees.'

'I'll try,' she said, determined to hide her inner flutterings.

They crossed the field at a leisurely walk, and as Lucy drew in deep breaths of the clear, crisp air she felt thankful for her jacket's protection against the sharpness of the southerly breeze which whipped colour into her cheeks.

By the time they had reached the third field she was beginning to feel more at ease in the saddle. The pleasure of the experience showed in the glow on her face, the sparkle in her eyes, and in the secret smile playing about the curve of her sweet and generous mouth.

Nor were these signs of delight lost on Silas, who sent covert glances in her direction. 'Enjoying it?' he drawled, his voice scarcely concealing his amusement.

'Oh, it's wonderful. . .' she exclaimed, beaming joyfully.

When they moved from one field to another he leaned

down to unlatch and open gates, and as the bay gelding went through the grey mare followed dutifully. Nearby ewes then ran away, followed by lambs that scampered after their mothers. Several cast sheep were found, lying on their backs while their legs kicked the air helplessly, but after Silas had grabbed their thick wool and jerked them to their feet they also ran, or staggered away, depending upon the length of time they had been cast.

They were in the fifth field near a copse of native trees when the incident occurred. Lucy had reached the stage of feeling relaxed, her eyes scanning the distant hills, her hands holding the reins lightly, when they came upon a rabbit lying in the grass.

It was almost under the mare's hoofs when it saw fit to leap into the air and then dart away at speed. The mare shied violently, jumping with a sudden jerk to the left with such force that Lucy's boots slid from the stirrups and she was thrown to the ground.

Silas was kneeling beside her in an instant, his face pale as he muttered huskily, 'Damned rabbits—they wait till you're almost upon them. Are you all right? Can you get up?'

'I—I think so,' she said shakily.

He helped her to her feet, then held her against him. 'No bones broken?' he asked anxiously. 'You can move your arms and legs without pain? Your back is OK?' One hand moved gently up and down her spine while the other arm continued to hold her closely.

She looked up at him, revelling in the feel of his arms about her, then said contritely, 'You must think I'm a prize idiot——'

He stared down into her eyes. 'Why should I think that? It's your first time on a horse, for Pete's sake. And please don't imagine that I haven't landed on my backside before today. It can happen to anyone.' Then he lowered his head and brushed his lips across her brow, her cheeks, until finally they found her mouth.

There was no way in which Lucy could control her response. Her heart thumped and her blood surged through her veins while her arms crept up and about his neck. The pressure of his tightening clasp caused her lips to part and her eyes to close. A daze of bliss engulfed her, and as her hand encountered the back of his head her fingers fondled the hair at the nape.

The action caused his kiss to deepen until suddenly, with what she sensed to be an effort of will, he appeared to pull himself together. His hands went to her shoulders, gripping them firmly, and as he put her away from him he said in a low voice that shook slightly, 'Do you know what one does when one falls off a horse? One mounts it again—*at once*.'

She looked at him blankly, conscious of the anticlimax that had brought her tumbling down from out of the clouds, then she nodded, while making an effort to convey the impression that his kiss had failed to have the slightest effect upon her.

Silas moved away from her, walking to where Misty nibbled the new spring growth with the utmost unconcern. Patting the mare, he said, 'She says she regrets the incident and asks you to forget it.'

The words sent a sudden hurt through her, causing her to regard him steadily as questions were dragged from her. 'Which incident, Silas? The first or the second? Are you speaking on behalf of Misty—or on behalf of yourself?'

He ignored the bluntness of the queries as he went on, 'Misty also says you are not to be nervous. Just climb aboard and she'll behave. She also thinks Peter Rabbit will have ordered the rest back to their burrows.'

She laughed, falling in with his mood while being legged up, but instead of forgetting the incident her mind was full of the moments she'd spent in his arms. Nor did she fail to take the hint that his only reason for the embrace had been to comfort her. And she also reminded herself that even if it had included a kiss it didn't mean a thing—especially as it had come from a man who was living in the outback to get away from women. And *that* was something else she'd be wise to remember.

After that long silences fell between them, and as they rode across the fields the thoughtful frown on Silas's brow made Lucy wonder if he regretted his offer of comfort by means of an embrace and—and a kiss.

It had been like this after the barbecue, she recalled. On that occasion she had put it down to the letter from Doreen, but now she began to wonder if the real cause of his irritation had stemmed from the fact that he had embraced her.

Nor was she very pleased with herself. There had been no need to cling to him with such ardour—no need to respond to his kiss with such wanton abandon. Her obvious enjoyment of every moment would tell him she was ready to go to bed with him the moment they reached home. Well—just you dare suggest it, Silas Wilder, she gritted inwardly. *Just you dare. . .*

It was almost lunchtime when they reached the home paddock. Silas led the way to the stables, where he unsaddled and attended to the horses; then he turned to her and said gruffly. 'You'd be wise to soak in a hot bath to ease your back and leg muscles. They are sure to be stiff after riding for the first time.'

It sounded suspiciously like a dismissal, but she made no comment as she left him finishing the task of putting away saddles and bridles. However, she realised the wisdom of his words, but hunger and the sound of the lunch bell caused her to discard all thoughts of a long soak, and instead of running a bath she stood beneath the soothing waters of a hot shower.

After that she put on a dress of burnt sienna which contrasted with her pale gold hair and made her feel more feminine. Nor did she skip hastily over her make-up, but avoided asking herself why she was taking so much care over her face and hair.

When she went to the dining-room she was disappointed to find only Matt sitting at the corner table, while of Silas there was no sign.

Matt sent an appraising eye over her. 'You're looking very—um—chic,' he remarked. 'Not at all as if you'd just dismounted from a horse. Silas told me he had been taking you round the sheep.'

'Where is he?' Despite herself, the question had to be asked.

'In the office, looking at accounts. I suspect he's arranging an afternoon of clerical work for you. I'm sure you'll understand we need to keep an account of all the food costs.'

'Yes—of course,' she said, recalling the barbecue.

'Ling will have a pile of accounts for you to contend with,' Matt said. 'He's meticulous in keeping the records straight.'

'I dare say I'll cope with them,' Lucy smiled, feeling thankful that her job in an accountancy office would enable her to do so, then, hurrying through her lunch, she went to the office, where she found Silas busy at the desk.

He glanced at her briefly as he said, 'I haven't checked the answering machine. Would you please do so?'

Lucy went to the machine and reversed the tape. The first voice made a request for permission to use the campsite area for a group of boys during the next school break, and after stopping the machine she made a note of the name and address to which she would send confirmation.

The tape was then continued, and after the first few words were uttered by the second voice Lucy almost froze in horror. Aunt Bertha was on the air.

'I *don't like* these answering machines,' her voice declared crossly. 'When I phone to speak to a person I like to *hear* that person at the other end. However—if I *must* leave a message I'd like *Miss Lucy Telford* to phone and tell me what I'm waiting to hear. She'll know who is speaking.'

'Will she indeed?' Silas queried softly while regarding Lucy with interest. 'Now what was all that about?'

Lucy felt embarrassed and more than a little annoyed with her aunt. 'It's—it's just something private,' she said at last.

'Private, huh. Who was that woman?'

'I said it's *private*,' she reminded him firmly.

'Obviously it's someone who knows you're here,' he pursued. 'Was it your mother?'

'Certainly not,' she snapped. 'Mother *never* uses such arrogant tones.'

'Arrogance being the operative force.' His lids narrowed as he became thoughtful. 'Actually, that voice reminded me of a certain warrior queen, so tell me— who the hell was it?'

Lucy put on a show of indignation. 'This is what I call harassment,' she complained sharply. 'I've no wish to discuss it, so may we change the subject?'

'Not until you've replayed that tape. I want to hear that voice again.' He left the desk and strode to the machine, manipulating it himself, almost as if he suspected she would refuse to do so.

Lucy listened to the repeated message with her heart in her mouth, and, hearing it again, the voice sounded even more arrogant than during the first recording.

As it ended Silas almost snarled, 'If that isn't Battleaxe Bertha I'm a monkey's uncle.'

'I wondered what you reminded me of,' Lucy snapped.

He gripped her by the shoulders and glared down into her face. 'Who is it?' he demanded.

She glared back at him. 'All I shall tell you is that she's somebody Mother knows.' Which was true, she consoled herself mentally. Then she went on, 'Matt said you have office work for me here. Do you want to explain it—or would you prefer that I pack my bag? I don't have to put up with my private affairs being pried into and dissected.'

'That is quite true,' he admitted drily. 'But if your private affairs were open and above board you wouldn't be worrying about having to conceal a phone caller's identity—which is what you are doing.' The words ended on a grim note, while a small frown drew his brows together as he regarded her.

Her voice shook with anger as she said, 'You're accusing me of being underhand?'

'I'll be frank. I've a strong suspicion you're being devious about something.'

'*Devious*? About what?' she demanded coldly.

'About your reason for being here. I can't quite fathom it. By your own admission you're not interested in the white-water rafting.'

She looked at him in silence.

'And you did not come for the horse trekking.'

Still she made no reply.

He went on relentlessly, 'You've come without gear for camping or fishing, and it's definitely the wrong time of the year for swimming in the river.'

'You're forgetting about my interest in a bush walk,' she pointed out, thankful to be able to latch on to some aspect of the place.

'*Bush walk*,' he sneered. 'If you stay here long enough you'll soon learn that it's rare for girls of your age to be even remotely interested in a bush walk. There's no excitement attached to it—unless it's with a male companion.'

'Ah, but my bush walk was with a male companion. Or have you forgotten——

He ignored the question as he went on, 'Bush walks are the preferred activity of older people—like groups from the Country Women's Institute, or the Townswomen's Guild or church groups.'

She could find nothing to say, and as she sat avoiding his eyes she realised she'd been a fool. She'd gone about this project in entirely the wrong manner. But if she'd been frank from the outset and had admitted to him that she'd been sent by his stepmother with the plea for him to visit her the result would have been short and sharp. Bertha would have been sent the message that she could go hopping sideways—while she herself would have been told to get down the road and out of his sight.

'So—why are you here, Miss Cornflower?' The words, gritted from behind tight lips, cut into Lucy's thoughts.

Desperately she tried to unscramble the confusion in her brain, searching in vain for a way to handle the situation, and it was sheer impulse that made her say, 'I came here to meet you—the wild man of the wilderness. Rumour has it he's getting wilder and wilder as time goes on—and I've never seen a wild man before. I just intended to take a quick look and then leave, but Stella's illness seemed to complicate my departure.'

He gave a shout of laughter, then said, 'My oath— you're an expert at finding an answer. If it's true that you were so keen to meet me I might satisfy your curiosity completely by reversing my rule to only date brunettes——'

He was interrupted by a polite cough that came from the doorway, and they turned to see Ling, who had arrived in time to hear Silas's last words. The Chinese, whose hair was partly grey, held papers in his hand. He favoured Lucy with a broad grin, laid the papers on the desk, then made a hasty exit.

Lucy had no intention of reverting to the former subject, so she said in a determined voice, 'I would like to get on with the job. What are these lists?' She lifted the papers Ling had left on the desk.

'They comprise Ling's housekeeping,' Silas informed

her, his cool tone indicating he knew perfectly well that she was dodging the previous issue. 'There will be a record of the meat he's used, the meat still in the freezers and what he thinks should be replaced. There'll also be a list of groceries to be purchased in town. The one for cleaning commodities will include those used in the chalets.'

'Housekeeping on a grand scale,' she smiled, making an effort to lighten the atmosphere between them. 'You'd better tell me what to do with Ling's lists, and after that I'll write a confirmation letter about the camping request.'

'And you have also a phone call to make,' he reminded her drily.

'I'll do that—later,' she replied, keeping her voice calm while checking to make sure the camping area was available at the required period.

'You mean you'll wait until I'm well out of earshot,' he gritted. 'Why do I get the feeling that the discussion will concern me?'

'Because your imagination has also gone wild,' she retorted.

He gripped her shoulders, shook her slightly, and glared down into her face. 'You are the most frustrating piece of womanhood I've met in a long time,' he rasped. The his head lowered as if he intended to kiss her, but instead of his lips finding her own he paused as though changing his mind. Then he released her abruptly and strode from the room.

Disappointment gripped her. He's furious with me, she thought. Nor has he taken the trouble to go into details concerning the clerical work to be done. No doubt he's putting me to the test to see how good I'll be at sorting it out. OK, Silas—I haven't worked in an accountant's office for nothing.

However, he was quite correct in assuming she would not contact the person who had phoned her until she was sure he was well out of the way, so she set to work in sorting out the various tasks to be done.

It was as she finished with the remainder of yesterday's mail that she glanced through the window in time to see Silas walking towards the stables. She snatched at the phone and pressed the buttons of her aunt's number, but there was no reply. And then she remembered that it was Sunday—which was her aunt's afternoon for visiting friends.

Irritated by the lost opportunity to speak to her aunt in private, she went to the typewriter and began on the letters of confirmation. After that there were cheques to be attended to and put aside to await Silas's signature. Nor were these small in number because, apart from the adventure activity accounts, there were also the farm accounts to be dealt with.

She worked steadily, determined to keep Silas shut from her mind, but despite her efforts he continued to creep back into it. And although she listened for the sound of his steps, she did not hear them. By late afternoon she realised he had no intention of returning to the office while she was in it, and she had a strong suspicion that he did not trust her. This thought was like a barb that hurt more than she cared to admit.

Later, when it was time for the evening meal, she entered the dining-room to find Silas and Matt seated at their corner table. They stood up as she approached, but there was no smile of greeting on the handsome face of the younger man. Nevertheless, he pulled out a chair for her.

Matt said, 'Silas says you've been busy in the office.'

So Silas had been discussing her, she thought resentfully. Had he been expressing his doubts about her to Matt? Somehow she felt this to be a fact, so she said, 'Yes—he's trusted me with such things as letters and accounts. However, the confirmations won't be sealed until he's checked them. I've already made one mistake by booking in a crowd on Ling's day off.'

Silas said nothing.

'I've a feeling we'll scramble over that hurdle,' Matt said drily.

Lucy went on, smiling sweetly at Silas as she said, 'And of course there's the letter from your girlfriend to be answered—the one in the mauve envelope that filled the office with perfume.'

'You exaggerate,' he snapped, frowning at his plate.

'Do I?' she queried innocently. 'Well, I'll leave you to answer that one because—with the letter hidden beside your heart—I'm unable to see the address.'

'You must have your little joke,' he gritted through tight lips.

She ignored his tone as she pointed out, 'The letter said this weekend, which isn't far away.' Then she smiled as enlightenment dawned. 'Of course—how silly of me—you intend to phone her yourself and enjoy a nice long chat. Just say the word and I'll vacate the office.'

Matt, who had suddenly become alert, demanded with interest, 'What girlfriend is this?'

Silas scowled at Lucy. 'Do you see what you've done? You've made his ears fly up like a donkey's.'

She turned to examine the older man. 'They look quite normal to me——'

'Thank you, my dear,' Matt said, then he spoke seriously to Silas. 'Am I to understand that you've heard from Doreen—and that she'll be here at the weekend?'

'What of it?' Silas demanded nonchalantly.

'Let me warn you, my boy—it's one thing to *look* like a donkey, but much easier to *act* like one.'

'You're suggesting I'll do so?' Silas drawled.

'It's possible,' Matt said quietly. 'Why is she coming here? I understand she has large ideas, but there's nothing grand or glamorous about this place.'

'Oh, yes, there is,' Lucy protested. 'It's different from

every other place, and it has an atmosphere that is entirely its own.' She hesitated, then said thoughtfully, 'Besides. . .couldn't she be coming because—because she has decided she really does love Silas?' She turned to Silas with an urgent reminder. 'Didn't you say she wants to take up where she'd left off?'

He regarded her coolly. 'The point is—do *I* want to take up where *I* left off?'

CHAPTER FIVE

MATT chuckled as he regarded Silas with an amused glint in eyes that were so like his nephew's. 'You might be wise to take a long weekend vacation—starting from before she arrives,' he advised.

Silas frowned at him. 'You're suggesting that I should run away from this woman?'

Lucy laughed teasingly. 'Would it be the first time? Isn't that what you did when you came here? Didn't you admit to me that you'd run away to the hills?'

Matt spoke to her earnestly. 'He came here to get away from *all* women. Nor have I any wish to see him caught by one who would drag him back to the city lights.'

She made no attempt to conceal her surprise, her eyes widening slightly as she said, 'You mean you think he should remain a *bachelor*—all his life?'

Matt returned her gaze steadily. 'It would be wiser— unless the right woman comes along. The right woman for Silas will want to stay here with him—and she must be ready to share the running of this place with him.'

'And of course she can forget the city lights,' Lucy added with a smile. 'Isn't that so?'

'No, it is not—it's utter nonsense,' Silas cut in sharply. 'When a show in town catches my fancy I go to it. And where do you imagine we collect our stores if not in the city? For Pete's sake—it's only about an hour's drive.'

Lucy said, 'In that case all you need is patience, and one day the right woman will come to you from out of the blue.'

'Or in a red Toyota,' Matt suggested mildly.

His words startled Lucy, forcing her to say with cold

dignity, 'I trust you don't imagine I'm here with the idea of setting my cap at Silas, because nothing is further from my intentions.'

Silas spoke with regret. 'Well, now—you disappoint me. What was it you said about coming specially to meet the wild man of the wilderness? It was just before Ling interrupted us—remember?'

She flushed while recalling her own words, although in a way they were true. She *had* come here to meet Silas, but definitely not to set her cap at him. At last she said, 'I was a fool to have made that idiotic statement. Surely you're not sufficiently naïve to have believed it?'

'So—you're admitting to having told me a blatant lie?'

'A completely shameless one. Sorry about that.' She giggled unrepentantly.

'I realised it lacked the ring of truth,' Silas said while regarding her intently. 'But I still get the feeling that you are here for a definite reason.'

'Yes,' she conceded reluctantly, knowing it was useless to deny it. Then she added, 'I've no intention of talking about it now, but I will tell you when the right moment occurs. After that I'll get out of your sight and disappear from your life.'

The right moment, she realised, would be when Stella returned. After that she would make her way back to her aunt, her mission a failure, because she now knew that in no way would Silas be persuaded to go cap in hand to Bertha.

Matt said in a tone of genuine regret, 'I'll be sorry to see you leave, but I suppose—eventually—you'd become bored with this place.'

She shook her head. 'To be honest I find it quite fascinating, nor could anyone become bored with so much activity going on. I—I just hope I'll be able to see a kiwi before I leave,' she added, a wistful note creeping into her voice.

'A kiwi,' Matt said musingly. 'Now that's our most famous native bird. In most places of the world New Zealanders are known as Kiwis, yet very few New Zealanders have actually seen a kiwi, especially in its natural habitat of the forest floor.'

'It's nocturnal,' Silas reminded him. 'People are not normally wandering about in the bush at night.'

Lucy sent Silas a side glance as she said, 'When I first arrived you said it might be arranged for me to see a kiwi, but I'll quite understand. . .' She fell silent.

'Understand what?' His brows rose as he turned his brown eyes upon her.

'That it'll be impossible, because your time will be taken up. Doreen will be here. She'll expect your full attention——'

Matt scowled. 'What she expects and what she gets could be two different things that are miles apart.'

'Oh, I think we can rely on them spending long periods together,' Lucy assured Matt. 'Silas must be given the opportunity to test his feelings for Doreen. After all, they were almost engaged. . .' She bit off further words, cursing her runaway tongue.

'How did you know that?' Silas snapped, his lids narrowing to slits. 'I don't recall mentioning that fact.'

'You didn't have to,' Lucy returned guilelessly. 'From what you told me I assumed it. Besides, you said she wants to take up where you both left off, so if that isn't a close association——'

Matt snorted as an oath escaped him. 'If he does that I'll *clobber* him—I'll *wring his neck*——'

Silas jeered at him. 'Huh—you and who else. . .?'

Lucy laid a hand on Matt's arm. 'You must allow Silas to work out his own destiny. Only he himself can decide where his happiness lies. If it's with Doreen—well, so be it.' She sighed, wondering why the mere thought of it made her feel depressed, then she turned to Silas and said hastily, 'So there's no need for you to worry about taking me to see a kiwi. I can go to one of those places in the town where they are shown to tourists in a specially darkened building.'

'You will not,' Silas declared firmly. 'I'll take you this evening. I know where there's a nest. Near it is a fallen tree where I've sat to watch the pair come and go.'

Lucy felt a surge of excitement, not only because here was the opportunity to see a kiwi in its natural surroundings, but also because she would be returning to the bush with Silas. At least she'd have a few precious moments alone with him before Doreen arrived. She pulled her thoughts together sharply. What on earth was getting into her? Of course they wouldn't be *precious*. Pleasant was a more applicable word, she told herself firmly.

They left in the utility a short time after darkness had fallen, and although little was said as they drove along the narrow, rough country road, Lucy felt that the silences between them were companionable. She also sensed that Silas was taking her to see the kiwi because it was something he himself enjoyed doing.

When they reached the edge of the bush he switched on a torch, and as they entered the opening in the trees they left the canopy of twinkling stars for the canopy of overhead branches. Before them stretched a tunnel of darkness, broken only by the beam of light that flashed over tree trunks and gleamed on the gracefully curving fronds of ferns.

A sudden fear gripped Lucy, and as she peered into the impenetrable shadows on either side she realised that the bush by day and the bush by night were two totally different places. And she also wondered why on earth she had desired to see a kiwi. 'It's—it's eerie in the bush at night,' she whispered a little shakily. 'It's so still—yet there's a breeze out in the open.'

'Why are you whispering? Are you afraid?' he asked casually.

'N-no—of course not,' she lied, irritated at being unable to keep the tremor from her voice.

'Give me your hand. There, now—does that feel better?'

'Yes—thank you, Silas. I'll admit I am a little nervous,' she added meekly, while becoming conscious that his firm grip seemed to send tingles up her arm.

He drew her against him, linking her arm in his as they walked along the track. His closeness gave her comfort, and she knew she wouldn't have dared to venture here alone—not even to see a thousand kiwis. However, as the torchlight danced ahead she gradually lost the worst of the fears that had at first threatened to turn her into a quivering jelly.

Eventually he paused to lead her along a side-track where the hanging vines reached out to cling about them. Yet he still held her hand, and she grasped it gratefully until they came to an open area where there was a fallen tree trunk.

He pointed the torch beam at the forest floor, which was littered with pieces of fallen bark, dried leaves and twigs, then moved it slowly towards a hole at the base of a tree trunk. 'There's a pair with a nest burrowed down there,' he said quietly. 'Can you see the egg?' He held the torch steady.

She peered into the nest, then whispered, 'Yes—it's a pale whitish green, and really quite large.'

'It'll weigh about a pound,' he informed her. 'In proportion to the kiwi's size the egg is the largest of any other bird. The male sits on the nest, but at the moment he appears to be out getting a meal. He never leaves it for long, so we'll sit on this tree trunk and await his return.'

As they settled themselves on the trunk Silas switched off the torch. 'We don't want the light to deter his return,' he remarked.

The intense darkness that wrapped itself about them

was like a black cloak that seemed to press upon them from all sides. It revived Lucy's fears, causing a shudder to escape her.

'You're cold?' Silas queried.

'A—a little,' she quavered. It was preferable to admitting she was again feeling nervous.

'Perhaps I could help you to feel warmer.' He unbuttoned his jacket and dragged her on to his knees. His coat fronts were pulled about her while he nursed her as though she were a small child. 'Is that better?' he murmured, pressing her head against his shoulder.

'Thank you—it's—it's marvellous,' she said with truth.

For several long moments they sat motionless, then his hand turned her face towards him, his fingers tilting her chin upwards. She felt his lips on her cheeks moving slowly across her features until they found her mouth. A sigh escaped her, and as she gave herself up to the pleasure of his embrace her arm rose to entwine about his neck.

At first it was a long, gentle kiss, but as it deepened it caused Lucy's heart to thump and her breath to quicken. She also knew it was affecting Silas because his arms had begun to clasp her even more tightly, with one hand moving to rest upon her breast.

But suddenly a tenseness seemed to grip him. His mouth left her lips and he muttered in her ear, 'He's coming. . .'

Momentarily bewildered, she whispered, 'Who? What?'

'The kiwi. He's coming back to the nest.'

'Oh.' The emotions mounting within her had made her forget the kiwi, and she now left his knee to sit on the tree trunk.

Silas said, 'Listen carefully and you'll hear him snuffling. He uses his long bill to probe for worms, grubs and other insects, and as his nostrils are at the tip he has to clear it by forcing out air.' He switched on the torch, but directed it upward so that there was only diffused light on the forest floor.

They sat and waited in silence, listening to the scuffling of leaves that drew steadily nearer, until suddenly the bird stepped from nearby undergrowth into the clearing.

Peering through the gloom, Lucy saw that it was about a foot high, its tailless, cone-shaped body covered with loose, shaggy hair-like brown plumage, tapering to a small head. A black, beady eye caught the light as it moved on short, powerful legs and toes, and as it crossed the clearing it paused for one brief moment to utter a shrill and prolonged, '*Kee. . .wee. . . .*' A few seconds later it had settled down into its burrow nest.

'Well, there you are—you've seen a kiwi,' Silas said.

'Thank you—I'm so grateful.' Was he about to kiss her again? she wondered. No—he was buttoning his jacket in a purposeful manner, and they were about to leave the scene. However, he continued to hold her hand on the walk back to the main track, where he again drew her close to his side while taking her arm. Looking up at him, she felt compelled to say, 'This is an evening I'll never forget.'

The torchlight betrayed his mirthless grin. 'You're sure about that? In time to come aren't you more likely to say, "Oh, yes—I've seen a kiwi, but I can't remember where—or with whom"?'

She felt dismayed. 'Is that what you want me to do?' she asked in a low voice, while savouring the memory of his kiss. 'Are you asking me to forget this—this hour in the bush?'

'I did not say that.' His reply came curtly.

'But you'd prefer that I should do so?' she persisted. 'Is this because of Doreen—because she'll soon be with you?'

'Why do you keep throwing her at me?' he gritted.

'I'm sorry—I don't mean to,' she said sadly, then
stifled a sigh while realising that slowly and surely he
was ruining what had been precious moments. Yes,
definitely *precious*—not just pleasant.

During the journey home she sat pondering this fact,
at the same time realising she must not allow her
thoughts to become emotionally involved with this devastating man. Evidently he was determined to walk
alone, and unless Doreen broke down his defences he
would become a replica of his uncle.

As for herself—she'd be a fool to fall in love with him.
It would mean returning to Wellington with a broken
heart, and despite their short acquaintance she already
knew it would be a long time before she would be able
to evict him from her thoughts.

Peering through the utility's windows, Lucy saw that
the fields were awash with moonlight, and, struck by the
ethereal beauty of the scene that basked in the pristine
freshness of high country air, she realised that this was a
property with something special about it. Nor was she
able to resist mentioning this fact.

'It's a dream place,' she said.

'You've noticed that much?' He sounded pleased.

'Who could miss all its delightful features?' She paused
for a few thoughtful moments, then said quietly, 'I can't
help wondering about the next owner.'

'*The next owner?* What do you mean?' His voice echoed
indignation while he sent her a sharp glance.

She hesitated momentarily before she said, 'I hope it
will be someone with *sons* to carry on the property. It
would be sad to see all your good work wasted, and the
place revert to its former wilderness. Unless, of course,
you imagine you'll live forever.'

'You're throwing Doreen at me again,' he growled
with suppressed anger while staring straight ahead.

The lights on the dashboard showed the scowl on his

face. 'Did I mention her name?' Lucy queried
innocently.

'No—but you dropped a dirty big hint that it's time I
was married,' he snapped tersely.

'I was thinking of the property, rather than of you and
Doreen,' she retorted, while silently admitting the truth
of his accusation. And then she found herself wondering
what had prompted her to utter remarks concerning his
private affairs. They had absolutely nothing to do with
herself, yet despite this fact she felt deeply interested in
them.

When they reached home he raised one dark eyebrow
and said, 'Milo or coffee? Ling allows me to invade the
kitchen after hours.'

'Does he, indeed? That's good of him, but—thank
you—I'm feeling rather tired. My muscles are reminding
me of this morning's ride and the unaccustomed exercise. . .' She broke off, hesitating to add that the evening's bush walk with its emotional upheaval was also
taking its toll.

She also had a strong suspicion that, despite his kisses,
Silas was thoroughly annoyed with her, and, while it
made her feel depressed, she felt there was little she
could do about it. Bed was what she needed. A deep
sleep to refresh her mind and to enable her to think more
clearly—especially about her own emotions.

Later, although savouring the warmth of the electric
blanket, she lay frowning in the darkness. Why, she
asked herself, was she allowing this magnetic package of
male virility to get under her skin, especially when she
hardly knew him?

Was it only Friday when she'd first set eyes on those
features that appealed to her so strongly? And was it
only yesterday when she'd worked beside him at the
barbecue while becoming vitally conscious of the attrac-
tion that made her feel drawn towards him? It was
unfortunate that Aunt Bertha had seen fit to phone so

soon. For heaven's sake—what did she expect? A mira-
cle? And now, despite the fact that he'd held her in his
arms, it needed little imagination to guess that he didn't
quite trust her.

Next morning Lucy found herself seated alone at the
corner table, and when Jean brought her breakfast she
learnt that Silas and Matt had left earlier to help the
farm manager move cattle into different fields. 'They
need fresh pastures,' the younger girl explained know-
ledgeably. 'Fortunately the spring rains have made the
grass grow, because the winter hay supply is almost
finished. But I don't suppose you know much about
farming.'

'One can always learn,' Lucy said gravely.

Jean looked at her thoughtfully. 'I don't believe you've
been out to see the chalets yet.'

'No—I really haven't had time.'

'They're quite cosy,' Jean informed her. 'When the
curtains are drawn across the windows they're very
private.' Then she added with an air of responsibility,
'It's my job to keep them in order. At the moment
they're unlocked, so you can look inside them if you
like.'

'Thank you. I'll find time this morning,' Lucy promised, sensing that Jean was seeking approval of the
manner in which she kept the chalets.

After breakfast she went to the office to continue with
the clerical work, but, before making a start, she tried to
phone her aunt. But again there was no reply, and she
decided that Bertha was either out in the garden or had
gone to town. After that she pushed the older woman
from her mind while concentrating upon several small
tasks, and at mid morning she took a break to follow the
covered path leading towards the chalets.

There was nothing elaborate about the small accommodation units, but, as Jean had said, they were cosy.

Bunks were set against the walls, kerosene heaters gave instant heat, while electric kettles enabled tea or coffee to be made. Brightly patterned bunk covers and matching curtains provided splashes of colour, and, having examined each one in turn, she was about to leave number four when Silas's voice spoke from the doorway.

'Well—what do you think of them?'

She swung round to face him, her cheeks flushing slightly. 'They appear to be very comfortable. I—I hope you don't think I'm—prying.'

'Why should I think that?' He sounded amused.

'Because I can sense you're feeling doubtful about me,' she admitted bluntly.

He looked at her in silence for several long moments, but instead of denying the accusation he said, 'As my acting hostess I expect you to know what they're like, otherwise it will be impossible for you to explain that honeymooners expecting luxury suites with king-sized beds will have to settle for a roll in the hay.'

'I'll do that,' she promised with mock seriousness. 'But isn't this the time of year when the hay is almost finished. What do I say when we're out of hay?'

His mouth twitched. 'You may inform them that the homestead's master bedroom boasts a king-sized bed which may be hired for a small consideration.'

'Very well—I'll do that,' she responded gravely, then asked, 'But where shall the master himself go to sleep?'

'I'll go to a small room along the passage.'

'You mean—the *toilet?*'

'Certainly not. I'm referring to a single bedroom not far from it.'

'Of course—the one with Doreen in it——'

'That's not the one I had in mind,' he said coolly.

'You're surely not referring to the one with me in it? Really—this conversation has become ridiculous.'

He sent her a level glance. 'You're saying I wouldn't be welcome?'

'Get this straight—you would not be welcome.'

He took a step towards her, gripped her shoulders, and stared down into her face. 'You can honestly say that after those kisses in the bush—that I wouldn't be welcome? Little girl, I could hear you calling to me loud and clear.'

Her face became suffused with colour. 'You heard only the kiwi,' she returned defiantly. 'Isn't that where his name comes from—kee-wee—kee-wee?'

'I see.' His tone became sardonic. 'So you're not honest enough to admit you're ready to be loved.'

'Everyone needs to be loved,' she returned quietly. 'It's just that I don't go in for casual encounters.'

He frowned. 'Casual——?'

'Of course. What else would it be? You seem to forget that I'll be leaving this place as soon as Stella is well enough to return to her job. Or even sooner,' she added as an afterthought.

'What do you mean by sooner?'

'Well, it's more than likely you'll want to arrange for Doreen to take over from me,' she pointed out as this thought began to seep into her mind, then she hastened to add, 'And speaking of the office work, I'd better go back and get on with the job.'

Silas gave a mirthless grin. 'You feel safer there, huh?'

'Safer from what?' she demanded coldly.

'Safer from the danger of my embrace. You're frightened of the feel of my arms about you. Why not be honest and admit it,' he jeered while blocking her exit from the doorway.

'Why? Because it's ridiculous, of course,' she retorted, yet knowing it to be a fact. 'Now, then, may we go. . .?'

He stood aside, and as they walked back to the office Lucy felt an unexpected wave of gratitude towards Doreen. In some strange way the thought of her arrival had become an intangible shield which protected her from making an idiot of herself. A fine fool she'd look if she allowed herself to be swept off her feet by more of those blood-stirring kisses, then found herself dropped like a burning coal the moment Doreen stepped through the door.

As they reached the office the phone began to ring. Silas strode towards it, then lifted the receiver. 'Hello, this is Wilder's Wilderness.' His eyes narrowed as he listened. 'Miss Lucy Telford? May I tell her who is calling?' A grim expression stole over his face. 'Her *aunt*? Hold the line—she's here.'

Lucy was unable to meet his eyes as she took the receiver from him. 'Hello—is that you Aunt?' Her voice shook slightly.

'Of course it's me—why haven't you phoned me before this?' Bertha almost bellowed from the other end.

'I have phoned you—twice—but there was no reply,' Lucy protested, making an effort to remain calm.

'Oh—well—I have been busy in the garden.' Bertha raised her voice. 'Now tell me—*is she there*?'

'Not yet,' Lucy replied, knowing she meant Doreen.

'Does that mean you're expecting her to arrive?'

'Yes.' Why had her aunt seen fit to ring at that moment? Lucy wondered, becoming conscious of apprehension.

'Must you be so brief? I suppose Silas is nearby and you're unable to talk freely. Is that it?'

'That's it exactly.'

'I thought you'd have brought him to me by now.' Bertha's voice had become complaining.

A laugh escaped Lucy, relieving some of her tension. 'As an optimist you take first prize, Aunt.'

'Why are you taking so long about it?' Bertha demanded.

'Because I'm working here for a short time. The hostess became ill and I'm standing in for her. I've explained it to Daddy.'

'*Hostess*? I wouldn't have thought a *wilderness* would warrant a hostess.' The words came scathingly.

'This one does.' Her aunt's tone annoyed Lucy to the extent of causing her to speak sharply. 'Please don't trouble to ring me again. You'll learn all I can tell you when the time comes and not a moment sooner. As for your request—I'm afraid you can forget about it. Goodbye Aunt Ber——' She bit off the last word and replaced the receiver, but it was too late. Silas was beside her.

'*Bertha*,' he rasped. 'I thought I recognised the royal tones of the battleaxe queen. So she's your aunt, eh?'

'I—I'm afraid so,' she admitted in a small voice.

'*Telford*—of course—I'd forgotten her sister's married name is Telford. I knew it rang a bell somewhere. Why didn't you tell me?' he gritted, his expression betraying disgust.

She recoiled from the look on his face. 'I—I just hadn't got round to it,' she said weakly.

'Well, you're round to it now, so what's all this about?' he demanded with suppressed anger. 'You should know that when people speak loudly on the phone their voice can often be heard by others in the room. I heard enough to learn I featured in the conversation. And I presume the *she* referred to is Doreen?'

'Yes.' Lucy knew that the time had come for her to admit to the reason for her visit. It was not the moment she would have chosen, but the determined glint in Silas's eye told her he expected to hear the truth. Nevertheless, she prevaricated as she said, 'Aunt Bertha has often thought of you—wondering if you're all right——'

'Huh—I can imagine it,' he scoffed. 'I can just see her dripping with tears of anxiety.'

Lucy ignored the remark. 'Actually she—she sent me to see that you *are* all right because—after all—you're her late husband's son and—and. . .' She fell silent, lost for words.

'You mean she sent you to *spy* on me,' he accused furiously.

'No—no—not really to spy,' Lucy protested.

'I can't think what else to call it,' he snapped. 'And no doubt she wants to know if Doreen is with me?'

'Well—yes—she did happen to—to wonder about that.' Lucy giggled as she added, 'She feared you might be living in sin.'

'So she sent you to find out. Is that all—or has she set some other task for you as well?' he demanded aggressively.

Lucy swallowed as she sent him a nervous glance. 'She—she wanted me to persuade you to visit her.'

He stared at her incredulously. 'I don't believe I'm hearing all this. If she's so anxious about my welfare and morals it's a wonder she hasn't come stamping up here to check out the situation for herself. She knows how to find this place.'

Lucy remained silent, searching for the right words to soften Bertha's attitude. 'She—er—she thought it would be *nice* for you to visit her,' she admitted at last.

Silas snorted. 'I can just hear her imperious tone, and I'm willing to bet that she said, "*He* shall come to *me*." Am I right? And I can almost see that aquiline nose in the air as the words were uttered—or hissed—or whatever.' He paused to glare at Lucy, before adding through tight lips, 'You can tell that old bag I'll see her stuffed before I move an inch in her direction.'

Lucy was shocked by his vehemence. 'My goodness, you are bitter. Obviously you don't know the meaning of the words "forgive and forget".'

Silas spoke quietly. 'Don't I? You do me an injustice. I'd feel differently if she'd made my father really happy, but, believe me, he soon learnt he'd made a mistake in marrying Bertha.'

'I suppose it was her bossiness——'

'He was an affectionate man, but she gave little in return. Now that he's gone she refers to him as her dear Tom. However, I can't expect you to understand how I feel.'

It was only family loyalty that prevented Lucy from admitting that her aunt's references to her dear Tom had never sounded convincing, and, giving a small sigh, she said, 'Perhaps I understand more than you realise.' She paused, looking at him thoughtfully as she went on, 'Now you know why I'm here. I've delivered the message, and I've received your answer. No doubt it's time for my departure.'

'No—I don't want you to leave, but I would like to know why you didn't tell me these things when you first arrived.'

'I felt I'd like to know you better before I broached the subject.'

His mouth twisted. 'Is that so? Then let me tell you I'm very disappointed in you. I consider you to have been two-faced and quite deceitful.'

Lucy felt stung. 'How dare you say such things?' she almost shrieked. 'I have not been two-faced——'

'Indeed you have,' he cut in bitterly. 'You knew, or could have guessed how I felt about my stepmother. The fact that she had to send you must have told you that, yet you came here without admitting your relationship to her. You settled in, posing as an ordinary guest.' His voice had become like flint.

She looked at him with amazement. 'Are you saying this place is barred to your stepmother's relatives?'

'Only those who plan the best way to entice me into territory I wish to avoid. Stella's illness must have been a godsend to you.'

Desperately, Lucy raised her voice. 'If you'd like to know the truth, I'd given up all thought of trying to persuade you to visit Bertha. It didn't take long to see it would be useless.'

'What brought you to that conclusion?'

'Yourself. I could see that you were hard and unforgiving. You're well-matched with Doreen, who was ready to kick an old lady out of the home she'd lived in for years.'

His mouth twisted. 'At least I'll say this for Doreen—there's no deceit about her. She's open and above-board. She says what she thinks, even if it is terse and to the point.'

'And no matter what hurt it gives to other people, I presume.' A laugh escaped her. 'That's Aunt Bertha's trouble. To me they sound as if they're very similar—so be warned. Marry Doreen and you'll be stepping out of the frying pan into the fire, as the saying goes.'

'I have no intention of marrying Doreen,' he declared coldly.

'No? I understood there was talk of taking up where you'd both left off,' she reminded him. 'It's my guess that the reunion really will take place—probably only a few minutes after her arrival.' The mere thought of it seemed to drag a blanket of depression about her shoulders, causing her to turn away from him and go to the desk. 'There are cheques ready for you to sign,' she said listlessly, making an effort to get away from the subject of Doreen.

However, further discussion concerning that lady was curtailed abruptly by the swishing sound of tyres drawing to a sudden halt on the gravel outside the reception entrance. The slam of a car door was followed by the tap-tapping of high heels on the steps and veranda, and then the bell on the desk echoed loudly.

Lucy went through the door to find herself facing a tall, dark-haired woman whose attire breathed sophisticated elegance. The dark eyes that swept over her were shadowed by heavily mascara-darkened lashes which contrasted with the white teeth gleaming from behind brilliantly red lips which were too thin for real beauty.

Even before the woman had opened her mouth Lucy guessed her identity, and this was confirmed when the newcomer spoke imperiously.

'Miss Doreen Andrews. Mr Wilder is expecting me.'

Lucy glanced down at the book lying open on the desk. 'I thought——' she began.

But her words were interrupted by Silas, who came from the main office. '*Doreen!*' he exclaimed, betraying surprise. 'Didn't your letter say you'd be here at the weekend?'

The thin red lips stretched into a smile. 'It did—but I couldn't wait. I just *had* to come earlier.' She walked round the end of the counter and clasped his arm. 'I know you'll find a nice cosy place in which to put me—preferably near your own room. Oh, Silas—*darling*—after all this time it's *wonderful* to see you again. We've so much to talk about—and so much to *plan.*'

CHAPTER SIX

DOREEN gazed up into Silas's face, her expression soulful, before she turned slowly to favour Lucy with a long and penetrating stare. There was a tense silence until she said, 'Silas, dear—who is this—this *person*?'

Silas introduced them. 'Lucy Telford—Doreen Andrews.' He drew a deep breath, then said with a faint curl to his lip, 'Lucy happens to be my stepmother's niece.' The last words came in a sardonic tone.

Doreen's delicate brows rose. '*Really*? Then what on earth is she doing here? I can see she's not a *guest*.'

'She *came* as a guest,' he said heavily, his voice echoing bitter accusation.

Lucy sent him a resentful glance while adding an explanation for her presence. 'My aunt sent me with an invitation for Silas to visit her. It's so long since she has seen him.'

Doreen made no secret of her amazement. 'Are you saying that Battling Bertha held out a hand of friendship?'

'Not exactly,' Silas put in grimly. 'She held out Lucy's hand, which is a slightly different matter.'

Doreen's dark eyes widened. 'What's got into her? If I remember correctly, neither of us were to cross her line of vision again, *ever*.'

Lucy said quickly, 'I think she misses Silas. She feels he should have realised she hadn't meant the things she said.' She looked from one to the other, glad to have got a word in on behalf of Aunt Bertha, but it brought no softening to the inscrutable expression on Silas's face. Indeed it was as though she hadn't spoken, because his attention appeared to be fully centred upon Doreen.

95

The latter beamed at him. 'How do I look—darling? Just as I've always looked?' she added archly. 'But perhaps you'd rather tell me later—in my suite. Please lead me to my suite—darling.'

Silas looked at her blankly. 'Suite——?'

'Of course. I always demand a suite,' Doreen assured him.

Lucy giggled as she thought of the small room next to her own. Doreen went on, 'Is there a porter or a steward to carry my bag from the car?'

'Definitely not,' Silas retorted crisply. 'The people who stay here carry their own bags. This is not a luxury Aussie skyscraper that caters for soft city folk—it's for those who relish a taste of adventure in the New Zealand outback. Didn't you know that fact?'

Doreen's nose wrinkled. 'It sounds very primitive. During the last three years I've become accustomed to refinement.'

Lucy smiled at her. 'Then I'm afraid you might not approve of our rustic environment and rural activities.'

Doreen spoke to Silas. 'Did somebody ask for Miss Telford's opinion? Please tell her I'm not at all interested. . .'

Silas ignored the comment and went out to the car to collect her case, returning with a particularly large one which hinted of a lengthy stay.

Lucy refused to take offence at Doreen's last remark. 'I'll check that there are towels in the room,' she said, then made her way along the passage. A quick glance showed that towels were needed, so she went to the linen cupboard and collected two large fluffy ones, but as she returned to the room the sound of Doreen's plaintive voice caused her to pause.

'You haven't said you're pleased to see me, Silas. You *are* pleased to see me—aren't you?'

'I'm always pleased to see old friends, Doreen.' His words reached Lucy's ears in a non-committal tone.

'This Miss Telford. . . Is she an old friend—perhaps somebody you'd previously met through your stepmother?'

'At least I can say I've met her through Bertha,' he retorted.

Lucy had no wish to be caught eavesdropping, so she walked into the room and hung the towels over the rail. 'I'm sure you'll find this room cosy, Miss Andrews,' she said, making an effort to sound affable. 'I'm in a similar one next door, and I find it to be quite adequate.'

'Perhaps you're not accustomed to real comfort,' Doreen suggested coolly. 'I suppose this one will have to do until I've had a look at the rest of the accommodation.'

Lucy sent her a level glance. 'Does that mean you'll be willing to pay for a more expensive room?'

Doreen's brows shot up. '*Pay*? I've no intention of *paying*——' She broke off and looked at Silas. 'Haven't you told her about *us*?'

He regarded her with amusement. 'What would you have me tell, Doreen?'

'That—that our relationship goes back a long way, of course.'

Lucy pointed out rapidly, 'It's not where a relationship has come from—it's where it's going that matters. Actually, I've heard a little about your relationship from my aunt—like the fact that you refused to accept Silas's ring until he'd kicked her out of the house.' She paused to draw a deep breath. 'However. . .speaking of accommodation, I'm afraid you'll not find any suites of the type you have in mind—although there are the chalets,' she added as an afterthought.

'Chalets?' Doreen was visibly interested.

Lucy sent a veiled glance towards Silas, who stood leaning against the dressing-table with an amused expression on his face. 'They're suitably equipped for the outdoor adventure type of person,' she informed

Doreen, 'but not for honeymooners. For instance, there are no double beds.'

'Oh—that is unfortunate,' Doreen said, her disappointment obvious.

Lucy went on, 'The only king-sized bed happens to be in Silas's room. At the moment he doesn't appear to be sharing it with anyone.'

Doreen cut in icily. 'Thank you, Miss Telford. That will be all. You may go,' she snapped.

Lucy went—and as she walked back to the office she wondered what had got into her to cause such unruliness of her tongue and to bring her claws to the surface. Why was she allowing Doreen to get under her skin in this manner? What did it matter to her if Silas made an idiot of himself over this woman? Yet she knew it did matter. Even at this moment, was he taking Doreen in his arms? The thought riled her, causing a rising anger which interfered with her work until voices made her aware that Silas and Doreen were standing beside the reception desk.

Doreen's reproachful tones reached Lucy's ears. 'Silas, darling—I've come all this way just to see you and to be with you. *Surely* you can spend the afternoon with me?'

'I'm afraid it's impossible, Doreen.' His voice rang with clipped determination. 'This afternoon four girls are coming to do a horse trek. They're members of a riding school, and I shall guide them over the route.'

The reply came petulantly. 'Haven't you *staff* who are capable of doing such mundane tasks?'

Silas's voice echoed impatience. 'Of course I have staff, but they'll be busy with sheep or cattle work, or attending to deer.'

Doreen sounded incredulous. 'My goodness—you are living a vastly different life.'

'That's because I'm a vastly different person,' he informed her curtly. 'From the moment Bertha married my father I was dominated by her. When I fought against it, the resulting unpleasantness always upset my father. And then in some subtle way I allowed myself to be dominated by you. But that's all in the past. I'm now my own man, and I intend to keep it that way.'

'Dear Silas,' Doreen cooed. 'You always did have strange ideas.'

'Did I? Well, I've now come to my senses, and it's as well for you to know how I feel right from the start. Now I'd better get the horses in.'

'Oh—well, I suppose I'll have to spend my time in just looking round the place.' Doreen sounded sulky.

'Yes—you do that,' Silas advised briskly. 'And if possible try to make amends for the rude way you spoke to Lucy. She came to my aid in a critical moment.'

A faint smile of satisfaction touched Lucy's lips as she heard Silas leave the reception office. So he had seen fit to consider her feelings. Or, on second thoughts, knowing that she could probably hear their conversation, was he sending her the message to disregard any idea that his kisses might have had meaning behind them? Of course—that was it. She'd come to his aid at a critical moment, and they were merely indications of his gratitude. She'd be an idiot to imagine anything else, she decided, while making her way to the filing cabinet.

And then Doreen's voice spoke from behind her. 'What, exactly, does this office job entail?' she demanded coldly while glancing round the room.

Lucy shrugged. 'Just the usual bookkeeping, except that here we are involved with two separate establishments. There are the farm accounts as well as those for the Wilderness adventures.'

'*Wilderness!*' Doreen's lip curled sneeringly as she uttered the word. 'It's a stupid name. It gives the impression of rough living, which is something I dislike. I'll make sure that Silas changes it.'

Lucy laughed. 'You'll have your work cut out to do that—to say nothing about having to contend with

Matt's opposition to the idea. Personally, I consider it echoes the atmosphere of the place.'

Doreen regarded her in silence for several long moments before she said, 'May I ask what qualifications you have to do this job?'

Again Lucy's shoulders lifted slightly. 'My years of experience in my father's accountancy firm. In any case, it's not my job. I'm merely standing in while Stella is having her appendix out.'

'*Stella*? Who is she? Tell me about her. How old is she? Is she married?' Doreen's questions came sharply.

Lucy smiled inwardly, guessing that Doreen sensed more opposition where Silas was concerned. 'Normally she's the hostess here. Her husband and grown-up daughter also work on the place. Do you intend making a bid for Stella's job?' she asked as an afterthought.

'It's more than possible,' Doreen admitted frankly.

'Are you sure you could do it?'

'Of course—with one hand tied behind my back.'

'How are you on barbecues?' Lucy queried. 'You'll need two hands for that particular job.'

Doreen looked at her blankly. 'Barbecues? I'm not very keen on them. I prefer to dine with dignity. What have barbecues to do with the job?'

'Stay here for long enough and you'll soon learn,' Lucy assured her while containing her amusement with difficulty.

Doreen moved about the office in a restless manner, giving the impression that she wanted to talk, yet not knowing how to begin. 'How long do you intend to stay here?' she asked at last.

'Until Stella returns and is well enough to resume work. At least, that is what I promised Silas——'

'A promise that was easy to make,' Doreen cut in, then added with confidence, 'I think you'll find yourself released from it quite soon.'

'That'll be up to Silas,' Lucy retorted. 'If it happens

I'll return to Aunt Bertha to tell her he is well and kept busy, and then I'll go home to Wellington.' The thought sent a wave of depression over her.

Doreen glanced at Lucy's ringless fingers. 'Of course you have a boyfriend in Wellington? No doubt he's anxiously awaiting your return.' She paused while watching Lucy expectantly, but when no affirmative reply came she persisted, 'I presume you *do* have a boyfriend?'

'Nobody in particular,' Lucy admitted casually.

'Then I trust you're not building any vain hopes regarding Silas,' Doreen warned sharply. 'If it hadn't been for your *ghastly* aunt we'd have been married by now.'

Lucy gave up all thought of getting on with her work. More than ever it seemed that Doreen wanted to discuss matters that niggled at her mind, even with a stranger, so she turned in her chair to face the other woman and said frankly, 'I don't see how you can blame my aunt. I understand it was your own stupidity in refusing to accept Silas's ring until he'd got her out of the house. I must say that such an attitude surprised me.'

'I was a fool,' Doreen admitted bitterly. 'I was a complete and utter idiot—but I wanted proof.'

Lucy was amazed to hear her condemn herself. She looked at her curiously, then asked, 'Proof of what, exactly?'

'Proof that Silas really loved me, and that I hadn't just become a *habit* with him. I needed to see him do something *special* to prove he loved me.' Doreen suddenly sounded pathetic.

'Like going out to kill a dragon? Only in this case you decided that putting an old lady out of her home would be a suitable gesture,' Lucy said scathingly. '*Charming*, I must say.'

Doreen spoke coldly. 'You know perfectly well that it is not really her home——'

Lucy cut in, 'You're forgetting that her husband looked upon it as her home and that he saw fit to make sure she had the right to live in it. He knew that if Silas wished to marry, the place was more than large enough for the three of you. Also, you'd have a built-in baby-sitter.'

Doreen's nose wrinkled with distaste. 'Actually I've decided against having children. The thought of soiled nappies and vomit on my clothes gives me the horrors. Besides, they clip your wings.'

'Then I doubt that you're the right person for Silas,' Lucy informed her. 'He'll need sons to carry on this place.'

'He won't be at this place,' Doreen assured her in a lofty tone. 'I'll persuade him to sell it and return to Hastings, where he'll take up his old life as an accountant.'

The statement brought a burst of laughter from Lucy. 'That'll be an interesting exercise,' she giggled, making an effort to control her mirth. Then, forcing a serious note into her voice, she asked, 'What happened after you'd refused his ring?'

'I went to Australia,' Doreen admitted, again becoming pathetic. 'I felt sure Silas would follow and plead with me to come back——'

'But he didn't?' Lucy queried quietly.

'No. So at last I've come to him,' Doreen said, then added in a firm tone, 'Nor will I tolerate interference in my plan to become Silas Wilder's wife.'

'Silas himself having no say in the matter? Tell me—why have you taken so long about it?'

Doreen made no reply. Instead she moved to the window and stood with her back towards Lucy. 'Mind your own business,' she said at last. 'My reason is—my own affair.'

Watching her, Lucy was struck by a sudden thought, her intuition causing her to say slyly, '*Affair* being the operative word. It's my guess that you had an affair in Australia, and *that's* what kept you so long.'

'What of it?' Doreen snapped over her shoulder. 'Would you expect me to live like a nun?'

Lucy's suspicions went further. 'But the affair went wrong—and *that's* what has brought you back across the Tasman. What was his name?'

'Clive. . .' The name seemed to slip out accidentally, and before Doreen could prevent it from floating into the room. Annoyed with herself, she drew a long hissing breath as she gritted through tight lips, 'Really, I don't know why I'm revealing all this to a complete stranger— somebody I've only just met——'

'It's the need to unburden yourself to someone who will listen,' Lucy said. And while she sounded sympathetic, she was in reality infuriated with Doreen. In fact she was so wrathful that her mind conjured a bleak picture of the situation. 'Shall I tell you what I really think?' she demanded.

Doreen tossed her head in an arrogant manner. 'I couldn't care less about what you think.'

'Nevertheless, I shall tell you. It seems plain to me that you don't love Silas. You're wrapped up in yourself. If you had ever loved him you'd have married him, despite Aunt Bertha's occupancy of the house. As for *Clive*—did he begin to look at somebody else?' she asked shrewdly.

Doreen went crimson with anger. 'How dare you make such a suggestion?' she snapped.

Lucy continued relentlessly. 'I'm not saying you aren't still quite attractive, but you must be creeping into your early thirties, so what you need is *security*—and that is what has brought you back to Silas. You made enquiries—you learnt he's still unmarried, and so here you are——' And then Silas's appearance at the door brought a halt to her flow of words.

'It's time you both came to lunch,' he said in a cool

voice. 'Matt is becoming impatient. He's ready to leave the table, but he's waiting to greet Doreen, whom he hasn't seen for years.'

'How sweet of him to remember me,' Doreen said effusively. She brushed past Lucy and took Silas's arm in a possessive manner. 'Let's go to him at once,' she added happily while beaming up into his face.

But there was no answering smile on Silas's face, and, watching him, Lucy thought she detected the suspicion of a grim line about his mobile mouth. Had he heard the accusations she'd thrown at Doreen? And, if so, would he recognise them as a warning that Doreen was not the right woman for him? Of this latter fact Lucy felt suddenly positive.

At the same time she doubted that Silas was the type of man who would stand listening outside a doorway, and although she recalled his firm declaration of having no intention of marrying Doreen it gave her small comfort. His mind could be changed, she reasoned within herself, especially if Doreen made an effort to charm him out of his present anti-female trend of thought. Nor was there any doubt of this being Doreen's first priority.

The thoughts swirled through her mind as she followed Silas and Doreen to the dining-room, and as they went towards the corner table Matt stood up. She noticed that his face remained unsmiling while greeting Doreen, and she wondered just how successful the dark-eyed woman would be in breaking down his underlying distrust of the female species. Nor were his first words to her encouraging.

'So you've come back,' he grunted in a tone that held little welcome. 'I must say you've taken your time about it.'

Doreen rose to the occasion by smiling radiantly as she said, 'I doubt that I've ever *really* been far away from Silas—at least I *know* I've always been in his thoughts.'

The older man's bushy grey brows rose as he shot her a penetrating glance. 'You must be a long-distance thought-reader, otherwise how would you know that to be a fact?'

Her answer came readily. 'Because he's Silas, of course. He's a one-woman man.' The veiled glance she sent Silas also swept Lucy, taking on a glitter of warning as it did so.

Matt changed the subject by turning to Silas with an abrupt query. 'This afternoon—I presume you'll be helping the men finish this morning's work?'

'I'll rejoin them as soon as the horse trekking is finished.'

'And tomorrow?' Matt pursued. 'Haven't we another rafting party?'

'We have—plus barbecue,' Silas replied.

'It sounds exciting,' Doreen exclaimed. 'May I join the party?'

'If you mean in the raft, you may not,' Silas drawled. 'But you may come to the barbecue.'

Lucy turned to Silas. 'Does that mean you'll not be needing me?' Then her heart sank as he grinned at Doreen.

'How are you on barbecues?' he queried in a casual tone.

'I've eaten at many, of course——'

'I mean on the cooking side of the job,' he explained patiently.

She laughed. 'Don't tell me you're expecting me to handle food for—for how many?'

'For about twenty or so.' The reply came nonchalantly.

Doreen laughed again. 'Darling Silas—you have to be joking. You *know* I don't like doing that sort of thing——'

Matt cut in with a comment. 'In this place everyone pulls his or her weight. During our last barbecue Lucy worked with a willing heart. Silas was delighted with her,' he added casually.

Doreen's lip curled as she said loftily. 'She's probably accustomed to menial work, whereas it's quite foreign to me.'

Lucy refused to take offence, yet her chin rose slightly as she spoke with a smile. 'I was glad to be able to help Silas. It was good fun to be working beside him. I really enjoyed it.'

Silas sent her a look she was unable to define, and even as she tried to fathom its meaning their gaze locked for several long moments until he reached across the table to squeeze her hand.

'I can only repeat my gratitude,' he said quietly.

His impulsive gesture caused Lucy's heart to skip several beats, and as she dragged her eyes from his hypnotic hold she became aware that, while Matt was grinning, Doreen looked anything but pleased. The latter's mouth had thinned, and her eyes glittered from behind narrowed lids. When she spoke her voice was charged with suspicion.

'You appear to have changed,' she declared icily to Silas. 'The man I knew three years ago would never have stood serving sausages to other people. I suppose you even wear a *pinny* of some sort,' she added scathingly.

Matt chuckled. 'That's right—only it's a plastic apron with trees and a large kiwi on it. It helps to remind the tourists of our native bush and that they're now out in the wilds.'

Doreen's voice remained cool. 'Do you think they *need* reminding, especially with all that *roughness* surrounding them?'

'What roughness?' Silas snapped. 'You haven't even seen the place. As for the man you knew three years ago—he is no longer around. Instead you see before you an individual who at last is his own boss and follows his own inclination. As for serving sausages—that task is normally in the hands of Stella and Bill Martin, whose absence compels me to step into the breach.'

Doreen realised she was going about matters in entirely the wrong way. She smiled sweetly at Silas, then said contritely, 'I'm so very sorry for anything I've said that has annoyed you. I didn't expect to find such a difference in you.'

During the conversation Jean had brought food and had placed it on the table before Lucy, Doreen and Silas, and now the latter laid down his fork while he regarded Doreen with infinite patience.

'You're missing the point of this entire venture, Doreen,' he said in a tone that indicated weariness. 'That roughness, as you're so pleased to call it, is what people come here to find. Day after day many of them sit at desks confined by four walls, their eyes glued to figures, their minds hassled by the problems of business. Naturally, they can't all come at weekends, so several get together to form parties for a mid-week break in the great outdoors. It gives me pleasure to be able to supply these adventures. It has become my hobby as well as my business.'

'But it seems such a terrible waste,' Doreen protested. 'You were a good accountant who had excellent prospects in the firm. I feel sure they were about to offer you a partnership.'

'That is something for which I no longer have the slightest desire,' he assured her. 'In this environment I feel free of all hampering trappings——'

'Such as the female of the species,' Lucy cut in, sending a significant glance towards Doreen.

The remark was met with a glare of anger from Doreen's dark eyes. 'What do you mean?' she demanded haughtily.

Lucy was already regretting her impulsive words, but, knowing she had to come up with an answer, she said in a matter-of-fact tone, 'Silas has already assured me that women will no longer play a part in his life. Isn't that so, Silas?' She turned questioning eyes towards him while a forced smile played about her lips.

But Silas ignored the question. He made short work of the remainder of his lunch, pushed his chair from the table, and stood up. His voice was brusque as he said, 'If you girls will excuse me I'll return to my job of preparing for this afternoon's horse trek.'

Matt also rose to his feet. 'I'll join you,' he mumbled hastily.

Doreen uttered a protest. 'But what about me? What shall I do with myself? Silas, dear—I've come here to spend time with you.'

A frown marred his handsome features as he turned to look at her, then he informed her gravely. 'I'm afraid you'll find it necessary to entertain yourself. I'll see you about six this evening.' And with that he left the room, closely followed by Matt.

Their departure caused a silence to fall between Lucy and Doreen, the latter sitting with an expression of sulky thoughtfulness on her face. It told Lucy she was depressed, causing her to feel a strange sympathy for the other woman, and at last she spoke with gentle understanding. Choosing her words with care, she said, 'Doreen—it's obvious you want Silas, but you also want him to be in the city. How you are going to get him there is not so obvious—so why don't you accept him as he is and with the surroundings he now loves?'

The reply came coldly. 'Because I don't love his surroundings. I want him to return to his old life, which I consider would be much better for him. While living here he's in danger of becoming thoroughly uncivilised.'

Lucy's eyes widened with indignation. 'Silas——? *Uncivilised*? Never,' she defended, then added thoughtfully, 'However, if you *do* get him back to his old city life, you'll know he's doing it for you, and you'll be assured that he really loves you.'

'Oh, I know *that* already,' Doreen exclaimed with confidence. 'It's just that he's suffering from a temporary loss of memory of our previous days—and nights—together.'

Lucy felt a stab of pain deep within her. 'You mean—when you went to bed with him?' she felt compelled to ask.

Doreen laughed. 'Heavens, no—I'm not quite so stupid. It's much more clever to play hard to get, because a man doesn't run after a bus once he's caught it.' She smiled complacently as she went on. 'Silas is still longing to go to bed with me, so you can wish me luck that I'll get him there eventually—but in the right circumstances, of course.'

A cloud seemed to descend upon Lucy, causing her to remain silent. In this matter she had no desire to wish Doreen luck, because the mere thought of Silas's naked body lying stretched in a bed beside Doreen's slim form only served to twist the knife that had stabbed at her previously.

Nor was the conversation doing anything other than drag down her spirits, so she brought it to a close by saying, 'I must go back to the office. If I were you I'd change those spike heels for walking shoes and explore the place. You might find it's not so rough after all.' And, without waiting for further comment from Doreen, she left the table.

But when she reached the office she found concentration to be almost impossible, and within a short time she became impatient with herself. Why are you concerning yourself about these matters? she queried mentally while staring at the typewriter. Silas's emotional affairs are not your problem, so why are you allowing them to snake about in your mind?

And then the answer shrieked at her all too clearly.

It's because you like him a little too much—or, to be honest, you're drawn to him a little too fiercely. The touch of his hand sends ripples quivering through your blood, his kiss is like an electric shock that sets your body on fire. Can this mean you're in love with him? No, of course not, you idiot. You've known him for only a few days, so that's impossible. Or is it?

That last thought caused her to pull herself together, and, making an effort to control her mind, she turned her attention to the letters to be answered. Summer was not far away, and its advent was bringing a variety of enquiries that concerned camping facilities, the quietness of the horses for new riders, the length of the rafting trips and the type of accommodation offered.

One woman had the temerity to ask whether a person would be available to dig up and carry the ferns she hoped to take away during a bush walk. The letter filled Lucy with indignation, and although she answered it politely she longed to ask whether the writer would agree to allowing a similar number of plants to be dug from her own property. But at least it had the effect of setting Lucy's mind back on a more even keel, and she worked steadily until she was disturbed by Doreen sweeping into the office.

Startled, she turned to discover the dark-haired woman glaring at her through eyes that were like burning coals. She noticed the tightness of the thin lips, instinct warning her that trouble was at hand, so she leaned back in her chair and waited for the storm to break. Within moments it had done so.

'Didn't you claim to be the hostess in this place?' Doreen demanded with iciness in her voice.

The question and tone with which it was uttered took Lucy by surprise. '*Acting* hostess,' she corrected. 'I'm standing in for Stella—as I've already told you.'

'Then it will have been *you* who decided I should be put in that small room next to your own. Well, I'm not satisfied with it—at least not while there are chalets standing empty.' She drew herself to her full height. 'I want a chalet and I intend to have one,' she declared imperiously.

'The chalets are kept for group bookings,' Lucy explained with as much patience as she could muster.

'But they are empty *now*,' Doreen argued.

'Didn't you hear Silas say there is a rafting party arriving tomorrow? The four chalets will be needed for sixteen men.'

Doreen's frustration made her quiver with agitation. 'Now you listen to me—if I can't have a chalet I must have a room where I can talk to Silas *privately*. Do you understand?' The words were hissed.

Lucy shrugged. 'You'll have to ask Silas about that. It was he who told me to see that the room was prepared for you.'

'I don't believe you. Silas would not want me to be in a room where somebody such as yourself could have an ear pressed to the wall. Can't you see that much for yourself?'

'No, I'm afraid I can't—and I'm also afraid that you might have to face up to the fact that Silas hasn't got private talks in mind,' Lucy pointed out gently. 'After all, you've been away for a long time, and you know the old saying——'

'What old saying?' Doreen snapped.

'The one about absence making the heart grow fonder of the girl next door,' Lucy quipped, the words slipping out before she could give them sufficient consideration.

'Yourself being the girl next door?' The query was full of suspicion. 'Silas said you'd been here only a few days.'

'That's right—only since last Friday,' Lucy assured her. She was already regretting her hasty words, which could make Doreen look upon her as a rival, when of course such a thought was ridiculous.

Or was it? she wondered, her memory reaching out to

the feel of Silas's arms holding her against him, and to his lips resting upon her own. Then she brushed the recollection aside firmly by turning again to the typewriter. 'You'll have to excuse me, Doreen, I have work to do,' she tossed over her shoulder while dragging her mind back to the woman who wanted ferns dug up during the bush walk.

Lucy did not see Doreen or Silas again until late in the afternoon when she moved to close the office window, and it was then that she caught sight of them standing outside one of the chalets. Even from the distance she could see Doreen clasping his arm while looking up into his face, and it was easy to guess that she was pleading to be moved into a chalet. Then, after they had moved into the small building, the door was closed.

Watching the door, Lucy stood waiting for them to emerge again, but their exit appeared to be taking a long time to eventuate. Doreen, she realised, was having the first of her private talks with Silas, and she longed to know if the barrier he had raised was about to crumble. However, she knew that she couldn't stand at the window indefinitely, so she left it to complete the task she had on hand.

Depression now wrapped itself about her, making concentration difficult, while the thought of Silas holding Doreen in his arms brought a sudden flare of honesty that caused her to admit she was jealous. And with her jealousy came anger that he could so easily hold her in a close embrace while he still had Doreen in his system.

Later, when she went to the dining-room, Lucy was still simmering with resentment, and she knew that unless she pulled herself together it would begin to show. She noticed that Doreen had a quiet smile playing about her thin lips, while the expression on Silas's face was entirely inscrutable. As for Matt, he appeared to be in a dour mood and with little to say. Has something upset him? Lucy wondered. Then, as if to answer her question, he pushed his chair back abruptly and left the table.

It occurred after Doreen had reached across the table to rest her hand on Silas's arm, 'Silas, darling,' she'd cooed sweetly. 'The chalets are so cosy. I couldn't possibly feel isolated in one of them—especially if someone came to see me,' she'd added archly.

Silas frowned, watching his uncle's departure. 'It's not your isolation that concerns me,' he informed her drily. 'There are times when we have unexpected arrivals, and then the chalets are required.'

Her eyes widened as she took on an air of great sadness. 'Does this mean you're giving more consideration to strangers than to *me*?'

'Not to strangers, but to the business, Doreen, especially when you already have an adequate room,' he pointed out wearily.

'But it's so small—and—and stuffy,' she persisted.

Lucy spoke quietly. 'Have you tried opening the window?'

'Mind your own damned business,' Doreen snapped at her.

Silas spoke harshly. 'This is Lucy's business. She's my hostess—in case you've forgotten that small fact. I happen to be more than grateful to her.'

Lucy regarded him thoughtfully. Grateful? But only on account of the smooth running of the business, she realised.

CHAPTER SEVEN

DOREEN continued to express discontent. 'OK—so she's your hostess for the moment. Must we discuss this—this accommodation question within hearing of one who is just *staff*?' she complained in an aggrieved tone.

'It was you who brought up the subject,' he pointed out crisply. 'In any case, Lucy happens to be someone who is more than just staff—as you put it. She came here as a guest, then offered a helping hand in an emergency.'

Doreen's lip curled. 'I'll bet she did. Really, Silas—I can't understand why you didn't call me at once. You knew I had returned from Australia, and you must have known I'd come immediately.'

'Nevertheless, you were still miles away in Hastings, while Lucy was here, right on the spot. And I must say I'd have been lost without her.'

The sincere ring in his voice filled Lucy with gratification, causing her to believe that he really did appreciate her efforts—on behalf of the business, of course. But—'more than just staff', he'd said, the memory of the words causing her to beam with pleasure.

Doreen sent her a shrewd glance, then spoke to Silas. 'Darling, you always were more than grateful for the smallest things that anyone did for you, but in future you'll be able to turn to me.' She paused before adding graciously. 'As for moving into a chalet, I'm prepared to forget it—at least for the moment. In the meantime I'll follow your wishes entirely.'

His mouth twisted into a wry grin as he said in a sardonic tone, 'Thank you, Doreen—that's mighty big of you.'

She hesitated, then said with the utmost sweetness, 'Do you mind if I make a suggestion? I think one of those chalets could do with an improvement.'

Silas looked at her warily. 'Improvement? What do you mean?'

She sent him a significant smile. 'Surely you realise that married couples like to sleep together—so at least one of the chalets should be equipped with a double bed.'

There was a momentary silence before he drawled, 'You think it would be a good plan, huh?'

Lucy also saw the plan Doreen had in mind, but she doubted that it had much to do with married couples in search of outdoor adventure. Obviously she had realised the futility of luring Silas into a chalet which lacked a double bed. It would do nothing to further her aim.

Doreen's dark eyes shone as she went on eagerly, 'You and I could drive to Hastings to choose one. It wouldn't take up too much room when the bunks have been taken away.'

There was a long silence while Silas stared at the table.

'We could go to Hastings tomorrow,' Doreen persisted.

'We could not,' he retorted sharply. 'You're forgetting we have a rafting and barbecue party tomorrow——'

Still she persisted even further. 'Then I'll go alone and choose one. I'll arrange to have it delivered——'

'You will not,' he barked at her with barely controlled fury. 'And kindly remember that I make the decisions around this place.'

Lucy sat back in her chair and shook with laughter. She had been waiting for Silas to assert himself and knew that sooner or later an outburst of authority must come from him.

Nor was Doreen slow to realise her mistake, her jaw sagging slightly as she said in a contrite tone, 'Yes—yes,

of course. Anything you say, Silas.' Then, as though
unable to keep her thoughts to herself, she added with
more force, 'I must say you've changed during the last
three years.'

'Is that a fact? In what way have I changed?' he asked
silkily.

'In your attitude towards me, of course,' she returned
in what sounded like a reproachful whimper.

A grim line appeared about his mouth. 'No, Doreen—
I have not changed. I've merely come to my senses
where women are concerned.'

His words were enough to throw Lucy into a state of
thoughtfulness, forcing her to become aware of how
impossible it would be to drag this man within yards of
his stepmother—and how futile it would be for herself
to harbour any emotional feelings towards him. Not that
she was admitting to anything more definite than a
quiver of tingling excitement every time he came near
her, of course. And as for recalling those moments of
being held in his arms. . .she'd be wise to forget them.

The depressing knowledge caused a sudden desire in
her to leave the table and to get away from the sight of
Doreen gazing soulfully at Silas. It forced her to push
back her chair with a muttered, 'Excuse me——'

'*Gladly*,' Doreen said with unconcealed relief.

Silas glanced at Lucy's plate. 'You haven't finished
your dessert,' he remarked sharply. 'Is there anything
wrong with it?'

'Of course not. It's just that I—I can't eat any more,'
she admitted while becoming aware of the misery growing within her and feeling perilously near tears. Then
she hurried from the room before they could rise and
trickle down her cheeks.

In her bedroom she buried her face in the pillow while
numerous sobs escaped her, shaking her slim body
uncontrollably. But at last she made an effort to pull
herself together, and, dragging herself from the bed, she

went to the wash-basin, where splashes of cold water to her eyes made her feel more normal. At last, in an effort to bring her mind back to an even keel, she went to the office, where she discovered a pile of farm accounts had been left on the desk. She dealt with them, then attended to various other tasks which kept her occupied for the remainder of the afternoon.

As the light faded she left the office and returned to her room, where she changed into a more attractive dress and attended to her make-up. Later, as she entered the dining-room, one glance at Doreen's model gown made her thankful she had done so. It was a black cleavage-revealing affair topped by a sparkling gold necklace, and with her hair swept up into a sophisticated style the older woman made Lucy feel like a country cousin.

However, neither Silas nor Matt appeared to be moved by Doreen's overdressed attire for this wilderness environment, and after flicking cursory glances at the low neckline they ignored it. But Lucy continued to feel uncomfortable, and despite the ease with which they discussed farm work and the moving of sheep and cattle to fresh pastures, she declined dessert and left the table before the others had finished their meal.

Restlessly, she returned to the office, then recalled that the answering machine had not been checked for several hours. She attended to it, to discover the only message on it was from Bill Martin.

Stella, he regretted to say, had had a slight setback. Her temperature was not falling as rapidly as had been expected, and this, he feared, had been caused by her determination to get out of bed too soon. Possibly she had pulled her stitches, or had developed an infection in them. Whatever the cause, her discharge from hospital would be delayed.

Lucy felt that the message should be relayed to Silas at once, so she went in search of him. A quick glance

into the dining-room showed he was no longer there, but
to her surprise she saw that Doreen and Matt were still
at the table.

She retraced her steps and the sight of the open front
door made her wonder if Silas had gone outside. Then,
staring across the moonlit yard, she saw his tall figure
standing at the top of the slope leading down to the
river. She crossed the yard and laid a hand on his arm.
'There's a message from Bill,' she said, then proceeded
to give him the details.

He stared at her intently, his face shadowed. 'You're
concerned about her delayed discharge from hospital?'
he asked.

She hesitated while searching for an answer that
would not betray the fact that she longed to remain in
Stella's place but that she feared for her own emotional
state.

'Well?' he demanded. 'Why the silence?'

'It's just that I—I thought you might want to make
alterations.'

His frown registered through the gloom. 'In what
way?' he demanded sharply.

She swallowed then admitted. 'I wondered if you'd
like Doreen to take over the office. She declares she's
more than capable of doing so.'

'Yes—no doubt she is—but what gave you the idea
that I have such a plan in mind?'

'Just your long association with her—also the thought
that your previous feelings for her could be reasserting
themselves.'

He stared at her thoughtfully, yet made no reply.

His silence encouraged her to be even more frank,
and, looking to where the moonlight caught the line of
his strong jaw, she said, 'I know you appreciate the help
I've given by stepping in to take Stella's place, and for
that reason I doubt that you would give me the sack—
or tell me to go. But if you'd like to give Doreen the job

I'd—I'd quite understand.' The words finished on a long, drawn breath while she waited for the words she had no wish to hear.

But they did not come. Instead Silas said, 'I think you've been working too hard. It's possible you're overtired—or even in need of fresh air.' And, having decided upon that fact, he took her arm and led her along a track she had not previously explored. It was bordered by tall tree ferns, with sufficient moonlight to show the way filtering through their high, curved umbrella fronds.

She looked up at him in a dazed manner. 'What are you talking about? I have *not* been working too hard——'

'No? Then what is this nonsense you're giving me?'

Irritation caused her to snap at him. 'It is not nonsense.'

'It's not? So when did I suggest that Doreen should take over the office? I have no recollection of it.'

'It's only a matter of time before you'll capitulate beneath the barrage of endearments. Silas, *dear*. . . Silas, *darling*. . . You positively lap them up like—like a tomcat with a saucer of cream.' Only after having uttered the words, which she immediately regretted, did Lucy realise just how much the constant endearments had riled her.

Silas stood still to stare at her in the dim light. 'I must say you amaze me. I had no idea you felt so strongly about the situation between Doreen and myself.'

Although annoyed with herself for having been so indiscreet, she was still unable to control her tongue as words slipped from her. 'I'm surprised that Doreen isn't out here now—strolling with you in the moonlight—instead of my humble self.'

He gave a short laugh. 'Actually, that was her intention, but she was waylaid by Matt. I think I told you that our families are old friends. Matt wanted to know how her parents had fared over the last few years, and as we were about to leave the table he asked her to stay and tell him about them. She had little option but to do so, nor do I think she was particularly amused.'

'And so you were out here waiting for her?' Lucy's voice had become scathing. 'She's expecting a moonlight tryst?'

'It's possible,' he admitted nonchalantly.

'If she finds me with you she'll have my eyes for marbles.'

'Lovely large blue shining ones. I know she's forceful, but I feel sure you'll cope with any unpleasantness she decides to throw at you.'

A sigh escaped Lucy. 'I'm afraid I'm not very clever at coping with unpleasantness—not even from my own relatives,' she said, thinking of her aunt. 'But if you consider I can cope—does that mean you think I'm also forceful?'

It was several long moments before he said, 'I've never met anyone quite like you, Miss Cornflower. When the sun shines through your hair it looks like a golden halo. It gives you the appearance of an angel.'

His words gave her a slight shock as they sent tingles of pleasure through her, but she knew she must not allow them to go to her head, so she pushed them aside as she uttered a light laugh and said, '*Me—an angel*? I'm afraid that's a long way from the truth.'

'You were an angel to step in when Stella became ill. You were also an angel at the barbecue.'

She stood still on the track, and, as she stared up at him, the shaft of moonlight slanting across her, her face betrayed surprise as she exclaimed, 'Silas—you amaze me. I understood you considered that act to be sheer deviousness on my part. You were positive it was an underhand method of persuading you to visit Aunt Bertha.'

'You felt I was harsh on you?'

'Harsh is an understatement. I shall never forget the

contempt you showered upon me. However, I realised it was your usual attitude towards women.'

'It might interest you to learn that I've changed my opinion on that matter,' he admitted drily.

'You're saying you no longer think I'm devious? Well, that's very big of you. Thank you—thank you very much indeed.' Her voice rang with bitterness.

He ignored her underlying anger as he said, 'And again you were an angel to make the attempt on behalf of Battleaxe Bertha, who is too damned arrogant to make the effort herself.'

Lucy remained silent, knowing this to be a fact, nor was there anything she could say that would make him feel more sympathetic towards her aunt. His encounters with her had been much closer than her own, and from an entirely different angle. Then, thinking of her own mother, she wondered how two sisters born of the same parents could be so different.

She was engrossed in these thoughts when a scuffle beneath her feet made her leap towards Silas and clasp his arm. 'What was that?' she gasped, peering down through the darkness.

'It was a hedgehog,' he said, the shaft of moonlight catching his grin. 'He was going quietly about the important business of searching for insects and worms when this great big foot came along and almost trod on him. It caused him to scuttle to the edge of the path and roll into a ball.'

'My feet are *not* big,' she retorted, somewhat aggrieved.

'They are to a hedgehog——'

'Nor would you have said such a thing to Doreen,' she lashed at him, feeling even more irritated. Then, realising she was still clinging to his arm, she snatched her hand away and moved to the other side of the path.

'Why are you so touchy about Doreen?' he asked with

barely concealed amusement. 'One would almost imagine you to be jealous.'

'*Jealous*——? Don't be stupid,' she hissed furiously, almost choking on the words. Then she tossed off a scornful laugh as she demanded haughtily, 'Why on earth should I be jealous of Doreen?'

He shrugged. 'Heaven alone knows—but—the lady doth protest too much, methinks.' His last words came in a soft murmur as he stepped across the path to clasp her arm and swing her round to face him. 'Are you intent upon quarrelling with me?'

'No—of course not——'

'Then let's nip this unpleasantness in the bud before it goes any further. . .'

Before she could be sure of his meaning his arms were about her, drawing her into a close embrace. His head lowered to find her lips, while any thought of resistance she might have had melted like an ice-block in boiling water. Despite herself, her arms crept about his neck, her fingers twining gently in the hair at the nape of his neck before moving to caress his cheek.

About them the world seemed to stand still, the silence broken only by the gentle rustling of the leaves in the branches above their heads. And although Lucy made a valiant effort to control her quickening breath, the mad thumping of her heart and the heated excitement rising within her, it was a losing battle—and at last she gave herself up to the rapturous bliss of the moment.

But like all such moments it came to an end, yet not before she had the satisfaction of knowing that she was not the only one affected. The message seeped through to her via the depth of his kisses, the gentle strength in the fingers that ruffled her hair before kneading their way down her spine—and his arousal, which betrayed his hunger to make love. His hand on her buttocks, crushing her against him, caused a strangled gasp to escape her, and it was that which brought these delicious moments to an end.

His hands moved to her shoulders to put her from him, then he released her abruptly before turning to walk along the path. No words passed between them, and as his strides lengthened she had to almost run to keep up with him. His haste gave her an uncanny feeling he was trying to escape from an unseen force—or perhaps from herself—and in her efforts to reach his side she panted breathlessly, 'Do you intend breaking into a gallop——?'

He stopped abruptly, swinging round to face her, the moonlight revealing his expression to be slightly bewildered. But, before he could speak, the sound of Doreen's voice floated through the night. It came from the direction of the front steps, the imperative note in her tone being unmistakable.

'Silas—where are you? Silas. . .?' The name was shrieked.

Lucy noticed the scowl on his face. 'You're being called, Silas. Your presence is required,' she said, unable to resist teasing him, and suppressing a giggle with difficulty.

But his reaction was difficult to define because he merely gave a small shrug and, taking Lucy's hand, he led her back along the path, where the darkness continued to be broken by the moon's rays filtering through the trees.

When they reached a gap he drew her through it towards the parking area, and there the sight of Doreen standing before the house threw Lucy into a state of gloomy depression. Still. . .those recent moments along the track had been wonderful—while they'd lasted—and she was learning to be thankful for small moments of joy.

Doreen hastened towards them, her face contorted with anger as she exclaimed, 'Silas—I've been searching everywhere for you. Why did you leave me with your silly old uncle? He was a *bore* with his stupid family questions—especially when I wanted to be with you. You could have *told* him to wait until tomorrow,' she protested.

'We shall all be busy tomorrow,' Silas reminded her. 'Surely it didn't hurt you to spare a few minutes for an old man?' His tone had developed an edge to it.

'A few minutes I *could* spare,' she flashed at him. 'But he went *on and on*, wanting to know this, that and the other. . .' She paused to glare at Lucy. 'In fact he held me up for so long I'm now wondering if it was a *deliberate* act on his part.'

'You must be raving,' Silas snorted. 'What on earth gives you such a stupid idea?'

'It was the chuckle he gave when I eventually dragged myself away. It was almost as though he's harbouring some silly plan for you—and *her*.'

'What makes you imagine such a thing?' Silas demanded sharply.

'The fact that you're out here with her now,' Doreen snapped, despite Lucy's presence. 'Is it possible your uncle would be pleased to see a closer association between you?' she demanded suspiciously.

Lucy found her tongue at last. She took a deep breath before storming angrily at Doreen, 'I don't have to listen to this sort of talk from you. If you must know—Silas and I took a short walk along the track——'

'"A short walk"—are you sure that's all?' Doreen sneered. 'What happened to your hair? It's a mess.'

Lucy was taken aback. 'My hair—what do you mean?'

'At dinner you didn't have a hair out of place—but now it's an unkempt, tumbled mess. Did it get caught up in the branches?' Doreen's voice was full of sarcasm.

Lucy said nothing, her mind in a whirl as she recalled the feel of Silas's fingers through her hair. The memory gave her confidence, and, savouring it, she held her head high as she spoke to Silas with quiet dignity. 'I'll leave you to enjoy the rest of the evening with your friend. Thank you for taking me for that delectable breath of fresh air—it's something I'll always remember.'

'You're sure of that?' he queried, his voice low and tense.

'Of course I'm sure,' she assured him sweetly. 'How could I possibly forget a walk that was so full of—er— *incident*?'

Doreen became agitated, her voice rising to a higher pitch as her eyes darted from Silas to Lucy. 'What is this incident—what are you talking about?' she demanded. 'I think you owe me an explanation, Silas.'

The domineering tones caused Lucy to pause before leaving them. How would Silas explain what she herself had referred to as an incident? she wondered, and, looking up at him, their gaze locked. Nor was there the slightest need to tell her of the thoughts that were uppermost in his mind.

Doreen's eyes continued to dart from one to the other; then she made an attempt to put Lucy in her place by reminding her that she was merely a member of the staff. 'You may go, Miss Telford,' she said imperiously. 'Mr Wilder and I have private matters to discuss.' She moved to take his arm while adding, 'Isn't that so— *darling*?'

'I'm unaware of anything of importance. . .' he began.

Lucy left them, conscious of a descending gloom as she walked towards the house without a backward glance. Would Silas take Doreen along that same secluded path? The thought caused an ache somewhere deep within her. Would he take Doreen in his arms and kiss her as he'd kissed her, Lucy? Spasms of jealousy writhed in her mind until she reminded herself that she had no right to object if he saw fit to do so.

When she reached the front door she was unable to resist turning to survey the parking area. Doreen and

Silas were still where she had left them, making two shadowy figures in the moonlight, and, even as she watched, they moved in the direction of the road that led towards the highway.

A sense of relief swept her, and later, as she prepared for bed, she told herself she was becoming too tense about this man. Surely she couldn't be falling in love with him? Could one fall in love in so short a time? The question kept her awake for several hours while she repeatedly reminded herself that it could only bring her heartache.

Next morning Lucy felt heavy-eyed and as though a dark cloud hung over her head. However, the latter was brushed aside when she recalled that this was a barbecue day and that she'd be working beside Silas. The thought sent her spirits soaring upwards, and she sprang out of bed to open the curtains and let in the early sunshine. The brilliance of the morning caused her to vow that Doreen would be unable to spoil that particular part of the day, and suddenly the last vestige of her previous depression vanished.

At breakfast she found no difficulty in putting on a bright face, directing most of her attention to Matt, who, for some unknown reason, appeared to be in a gloomy mood, and who had little to say in response to her cheerful remarks.

However, it was Silas who really puzzled her, his attitude towards Doreen being one of exaggerated kindly understanding, which gave the impression he was humouring a spoilt child. But Doreen retained the sulkiness she'd brought to the table, and when Jean placed fruit and cereal before her there was not the slightest sign of a polite thank-you. Had last night's evening walk ended in a quarrel? Lucy wondered, while noticing that the silences at the table were becoming painful.

In an effort to break one of them she forced a smile as she spoke to Doreen. 'Are you coming to the barbecue with us today—or are you going to Hastings to choose a double bed?'

The question brought Matt to life. '*Double bed*? What nonsense is this about a double bed?' he demanded, his eyes switching from Doreen to Lucy.

'I thought it would be an asset in one of the chalets,' Doreen explained, with a reproachful glance thrown at Silas.

Matt snorted, then glared at Silas. 'Have you taken leave of your senses——?'

Silas's mouth twitched. 'Not quite. I think that Doreen now understands that a double bed will not fit into any of the chalets.'

Doreen looked at him pleadingly as she persisted, 'I thought it would be so nice for—for married couples——'

Matt sent her a penetrating stare. 'So it was *your* idea? Then let me assure you that couples who come here—married or otherwise—get their exercise outdoors rather than in bed.'

Lucy watched the slow flush creeping into Doreen's cheeks, and felt sorry for her. It was easy to guess that last evening's walk had not been a success. No doubt dissension had been caused by Doreen's determination to see a double bed installed in one of the chalets—coupled with Silas's equal determination that it would not happen. Couldn't she see that this was not the same Silas she'd known three years ago?

At last Lucy said, 'Then you'll be coming to the barbecue. . .?'

Doreen sent her a cool glance. 'Of course. But don't imagine I'll be cooking sausages—or anything else, for that matter. That job is all yours and you're more than welcome to it.'

Lucy smiled, but said nothing. She had no intention

of allowing these people to know how happy she would be working beside Silas—nor must Silas himself be given an inkling of her inner joy.

And then Silas echoed his own satisfaction as he said, 'Lucy and I shall manage nicely, thank you. We've done it before.'

Matt turned to Doreen, peering at her from beneath his bushy brows. 'So how shall your time be filled in at the barbecue?' he queried with an unmistakable edge to his voice.

She sent an oblique glance towards Silas, then said casually, 'Oh, I'll probably chat brightly to entertain the raft parties when they arrive—which is what a good hostess should be doing.'

Matt stood up. 'Well—that should prove to be an interesting surprise for all,' he snorted as he left the table.

Doreen's dark eyes glittered slightly as she watched the older man's tall figure cross the room. 'What's the matter with him? Why doesn't he like me? I *know* he doesn't like me. Silas, darling—haven't you told him that we're together again?'

'The subject has not yet come up,' Silas drawled.

Lucy flashed a startled glance at him. Would the subject come up? Did he intend to renew his old association with Doreen? The thought gave her a pain, yet she forced herself to smile as she said in a steady voice, 'I hope you'll both be very happy.'

He looked at her gravely. 'Thank you, Lucy. I'm merely taking your advice.'

She frowned, feeling slightly bewildered. 'My—my advice?'

'Don't you recall impressing upon me the importance of giving myself time to make sure——'

She bit her lip as her own words flung themselves back in her face. 'You're not giving yourself a chance to

test your own feelings', she had advised. And now he
was doing just that.

Doreen snapped impatiently, 'What are you talking
about? Why should you take *her* advice when you have
me to turn to?'

'Why? Because Lucy has been a tower of strength,' he
informed her candidly. 'When I needed help she was
there to stand beside me.'

'So what?' Doreen demanded angrily. 'I'm here now—
to stand beside you—and I'll thank you to remember
it.'

'Then you can do so today—*at the barbecue*,' Lucy
hissed, suddenly infuriated with them both, although
more so with Silas than with Doreen. Surely he'd had
time to see the latter clearly?

'What is this?' he gritted at Lucy. 'Are you bowing
out?'

'I'm giving *her* the chance to show what *she* can do,'
Lucy retorted, then left the table before tears of frustration could betray the bitter hurt raging within her.

All too clearly the reason for last evening's kisses
registered in her mind, and as she hastened towards the
office she mumbled audibly to herself, 'Blast you, Silas
Wilder—you think you're vastly smart—you think
you're so confoundedly devastating that a few kisses will
keep me happily at your side—ready and willing to slave
over your wretched barbecue. That's all those kisses
were about—nothing more and nothing less. You can't
fool me on that score.'

The monologue came to an end when she reached the
office, where she slammed the door, then leaned against
it while trying to clear the anger from her mind. But the
more she thought of Silas's kisses the more infuriated
she became, and as she recalled her own response her
fury turned to bitter humiliation.

Eventually she simmered down sufficiently to complete a few small office jobs, and she had just checked

the answering machine when the sound of voices floated through the open front entrance. One glance at the young men emerging from a vehicle told her that the rafting parties had arrived, and within moments Silas was there to greet them.

Doreen was also there, gushing girlishly and doing her best to chat affably with various members of the group. However, they paid little or no attention to her, and Lucy guessed that their minds were too occupied with the exciting venture which would take them down the foaming white waters of the river.

She then saw the men turn and make their way to where she stood on the veranda, and she knew that Silas had sent them to sign the register. As they approached, she recognised the leader of the group as being one who had been with the previous rafting party.

He grinned and spoke to her cheerfully. 'Hi—remember me? I'm glad to see you're still here. That dame over there told us that she is now the hostess. Is that true?'

Lucy felt startled, but forced herself to remain calm. 'If she is, I haven't yet been told about it,' she said, forcing a smile. Had Silas made these arrangements? she wondered miserably—and if so, wouldn't he have told her? Feeling dejected, she tried to push the questions from her mind, and as soon as the register formalities had been completed she left the office and went to see if she could assist Matt with the loading of the barbecue trailer.

The old man straightened his back after making sure the trailer was securely attached to the rear of the minibus. 'Be a dear girl and check that Ling has the hampers ready,' he said.

In the kitchen she found Ling busily filling the two food hampers, but when she offered to help his refusal was firm but polite.

'No, thank you, miss—I like to do the job myself, and then I know that nothing has been left out.'

She watched as he closed a lid. 'You're so very efficient, Ling,' she complimented him. 'I don't know how this place would carry on without you.'

The small man's shoulders lifted in a slight shrug. 'Nobody is irreplaceable, miss,' he remarked nonchalantly. 'Not you—not me.'

'I suppose you're right,' Lucy sighed, knowing that she herself could be replaced by Doreen within moments of Silas's discovering that he did care for his ex-girlfriend after all.

Ling buckled the straps of another hamper. 'There, now—that should fill the bellies of those young fellows,' he remarked with satisfaction. 'They'll make short work of it at the end of their river trip.'

'They have a lovely day for it,' Lucy remarked while staring through the kitchen window. 'The sky is clear and the sun is shining brightly.'

Ling was thoughtful before he said, 'So you think it will stay that way? In China we have an old proverb which says, "Never judge the day by the morning". Sun might shine in the morning, but by afternoon the clouds can have gathered'.

'You make that sound like an omen, Ling,' she said lightly, at the same time wondering why the words made her feel despondent.

He remained grave. 'Clouds drop on shoulders of people. They fall unexpectedly from out of the blue.'

'We call that rain.' She smiled. 'You know perfectly well that the earth needs rain—and then the sun comes again.' She looked at him thoughtfully, wondering if he had something on his mind.

His next words seemed to confirm this. 'That woman friend of the boss who clings to his arm in the moonlight—do you think she will stay here for a long time?'

Lucy was shocked. '*Ling*—were you spying on them?'

His answer came with cold dignity. 'Ling does not need to spy. Last night I drive in my little old car to return a book to the farm manager. When I return my headlights sweep over the boss and this woman.' He paused before adding significantly, 'My eyes don't miss much. So how long you think she stay?'

Lucy was surprised by his interest. 'Do I detect a faint reservation in your attitude towards Doreen?' she asked, watching him closely and wondering if he would confide in her.

The reply came frankly. 'She treats me with disdain. It means that I can smell disruption.'

She drew a deep breath. 'Then you had better be prepared for disruption, because I fear she could be here permanently.'

His eyes widened a fraction. 'You *fear*? Ah—*I thought so*.'

Lucy felt colour rising to her cheeks. 'You thought what?'

'You're in love with the boss.'

She went a deeper red. 'Nonsense. You go too far, Ling.'

'Do I? You're sure about that? You take a good look inside your heart and you'll see the image of the boss.'

A hot denial rose to Lucy's lips, but before it could be uttered Silas and Matt entered the kitchen to collect the hampers. She followed them meekly, avoiding Ling's watchful eyes as she left the room, although she was well aware of his wide grin.

He's got a nerve to make such comments, Lucy told herself crossly. Of course he's absolutely *wrong*, she decided with a surge of irritation.

CHAPTER EIGHT

WITHIN moments of leaving the kitchen, Lucy's annoyance was stirred to an even greater degree when she discovered Doreen already settled in the minibus that would be driven by Silas.

The dark eyes swept her with a triumphant gleam as the other woman said smugly, 'Silas said I was to sit beside him.'

Lucy licked dry lips. 'I'm quite sure that he did,' she said.

'You're quite sure who did what?' Silas drawled from behind her, regarding Lucy with interest.

But before Lucy could answer Doreen leaned forward and lied in a sweet voice, 'I told Miss Telford that you'd said for her to get into the bus. She said she felt sure you'd want me to sit beside you.'

Silas sent Lucy a bleak look as he said crisply, 'Well—aren't you getting in? There's room for three in the front seat.'

Her eyes had become shadowed by dejection. 'No doubt there is—but I shall travel with Matt.'

'Yes, you do that,' Doreen chimed in eagerly. 'It's stupid to have three crammed into one seat while dear old Matt travels alone.'

Lucy made no reply as she turned away and went to where Matt was placing zipper bags of clothing for the men into the minibus. She looked at him wistfully, then asked, 'Please may I travel with you?'

He sent her a long, steady look, then glanced across the yard. 'Get in, lass,' was all he said.

She climbed into the front seat, grateful that she did not have to sit beside Doreen, who would be sure to take the opportunity of snuggling up to Silas. She felt depressed, and only with an effort was she able to chat to Matt with any degree of cheerfulness.

But this was achieved only because she happened to be a good listener, and, after a few leading questions about his earlier life in the high, mountainous country of the South Island, he talked almost non-stop. The journey was taken at a leisurely pace because of the trailer, yet, despite her dejection, Matt's reminiscences caused it to pass rapidly.

When they reached the shearers' quarters she became a bundle of activity, doing all she could to assist Matt in setting up the large barbecue, and then searching for dry wood to boil the water for the billy tea.

'You're a grand little worker,' he observed, watching her vigorous movements in washing the long table where the rafting party would sit. 'Those tables are OK—you did them before we left only last Saturday.'

'Oh, I like to be busy,' she said evasively. How could she admit she was becoming agitated because Silas and Doreen had not yet appeared? They couldn't have been so very far behind them—in fact they should have passed them unless—unless Silas had decided to turn along the road that would take them to the bush walk. Would he kiss Doreen beneath the shelter of the tall trees? The thought caused her to quiver with a surge of jealousy that swept through her with frightening force.

Matt said casually, 'I think Silas intended going to the bush.'

'Oh——?' The exclamation escaped her as a startled squeak. Had he read her thoughts?

Matt went on, 'There's a bridge that needs attention. It has to be extended on either side of the stream, so he has to take a note of the timber required. We can't have people falling into the stream, even if it isn't deep.'

'Oh, yes—I remember that place where the bank has been washed away.' But even more vividly she recalled her own fall and Silas's swift leap across the narrow stream to sweep her up into his arms. Dreamily, she stood gazing into space while reliving those moments, until Matt's voice hit her ears.

'I suppose you'll be gathering more snowdrops. I notice there are still a few out there.' He coughed, then added almost grudgingly, 'I thought they gave a feminine touch to the table.'

'You're saying you approve of feminine touches?' she shot at him, placing a pile of plates on the end of the table. Then, unable to hold back the words, she added, 'I've been given to understand that you and Silas are both somewhat allergic to—er—to the feminine side of life—and that you've both decided to live without such small luxuries.'

There was a lengthy pause before he admitted, 'An unhappy experience in my younger days made me too dogmatic about certain ideas that became stuck in my head. I don't want Silas to make the same mistake.' The words came reluctantly, almost as if they were being dragged from him.

Her blue eyes widened with surprise. 'You're actually saying you made a mistake in keeping women out of your life?'

'There are times when women have a place in a man's life,' he admitted gruffly.

She felt a prickle of resentment as she said, 'I suppose you mean for washing. . .ironing. . .cooking. . .and *sleeping*, of course. I thought women could be hired for those services.'

He shook his head. 'True love and companionship can never be hired. Nor can they be bought.'

'Does this mean that you approve of Silas's alliance with Doreen?' she asked, making an effort to keep the dismay from her voice.

'I didn't say that,' he retorted stiffly. 'I simply meant that if Silas finds himself in love with a woman who loves him in return, he must make her his own. Nature must take its course without interference from an old man such as myself.'

'I suppose you're right,' she sighed, then took the jar from the shelf and filled it with water before going out to pick snowdrops.

There were still plenty to be found, and she had almost finished arranging them when the second minibus arrived. She heard Silas's deep tones speaking to Matt, who happened to be standing near the door, and then a derisive laugh came from behind her as Doreen entered the shearers' quarters.

'*Snowdrops*?' she sneered. 'Are you trying to impress somebody? Could it be Silas—or the men in the rafts—or perhaps it's one of the guides?' she finished waspishly.

A slow flush crept into Lucy's cheeks, but she controlled herself while putting the last of the long, slim leaves into position, then she turned slowly to face the other woman. Staring at her wordlessly, she noticed that Doreen's lips appeared to be thinner than usual, and that her eyes held a glitter that betrayed subdued anger.

At last she queried in a calm voice, 'What's the matter with you, Doreen? Why are you so—*bitchy*? Didn't you go for a lovely bush walk to measure timber for the bridge? Didn't you get all you'd hoped for?' The last question was uttered in a guileless manner.

'What do you know about bush walks?' Doreen demanded, staring at Lucy suspiciously. 'Hasn't the job kept you too busy for aimless wandering among trees?'

'Not at all. Silas has taken me there twice.' A broad smile spread over Lucy's face as she recalled the occasions.

'*Twice*?' Doreen drew a sharp breath.

Lucy nodded. 'During the first walk we saw a weka, but the second time was much more exciting because we sat on a log and waited for a kiwi to return to its nest.'

The dark eyes narrowed. 'Kiwis are nocturnal birds—

so that means you must have been there at night. You were out there with Silas—after dark?'

Lucy nodded, her flush deepening while memory caused her eyes to shine. 'Yes—it was wonderful,' she sighed rapturously.

Doreen's eyes became slits that rivalled Ling's as they scanned Lucy's tell-tale face. '*Did he kiss you*—out there in the dark?' The words were hissed.

'Why don't you ask him about that?' Lucy suggested, turning away from her.

Doreen grabbed her arm, swinging her round to face her again. 'I'm asking *you*—I demand to know—*did he kiss you?*' Her voice had become raised to a high-pitched shriek of anger.

The sound of it brought Silas into the shearers' quarters. 'What is going on?' he rasped, his glance darting from one to the other.

Doreen dropped Lucy's arm. She sent Silas a baleful glare, then, ignoring his question, she brushed past him to leave the room.

Silas watched her go, then turned to Lucy. 'Perhaps you'll be good enough to enlighten me. What was all that about? It's useless to deny there's been a quarrel. What were you talking about?'

'Bush walks,' Lucy informed him briefly, rubbing the arm that had been clawed by Doreen.

'How could you quarrel over a bush walk?' he pursued.

Lucy knew she had to tell him something, so she said, 'She got mad with me when I admitted you'd taken me for two bush walks. She wanted to know if—if you'd kissed me.' Despite herself, the words were dragged from her.

'I can almost hear your reply,' he retorted mockingly. 'I can imagine you saying that you really couldn't tell her because you'd entirely forgotten the incident—and if it *had* occurred it meant nothing to you.'

She felt stung by his reply. 'No doubt that is what you *hope* I said. Sheer wishful thinking. Please don't bother to deny it—you've made it more than obvious.' Her voice shook, echoing dismay as she stared at him, wide-eyed.

'Well, what *did* you say?' he persisted.

'I told her to ask you—so why don't you rush after her right now? Take her in your arms and tell her you love her.' The last words came so vehemently that she almost choked on them.

He stared at her in amazement, then again mocked, 'My goodness—we are in a state of tizziness.'

'It's nothing to the tizz we'll be in if we don't get that barbecue working,' she snapped, then went to examine the contents of the hampers. The remainder of the plates were taken to be placed on the table, and she began rolling the cutlery into paper napkins, her fingers shaking as she did so.

If he noticed this fact he made no comment. Instead he said, 'Why don't you ask Doreen to attend to that small task while you sort out the food? The raft parties will be here soon. They got away earlier than usual, and the river is suitable for a fairly fast run.'

Lucy lifted her head and glared at him. 'Why don't *you* ask *her* to sort out the food? I'm sure you'd prefer *her* to work beside you.'

'You're wrong,' he rasped. 'I want you to work beside me. Surely I've made that point clear enough.'

For a moment her heart stood still, then her lip trembled as she spoke tremulously. 'That's only because you know I'll be more efficient at the job. But now is your big opportunity to begin training *her* as your chief assistant.'

He ran long fingers through his dark hair in a gesture of extreme exasperation. 'For Pete's sake—what's got into you? Have you forgotten she has no wish to be involved with the barbecue? Why are you making things so difficult? Last time I actually imagined you enjoyed working beside me. I must have been mistaken.'

She looked at him wordlessly, unable to find an answer to his first question. What, indeed, had got into her? She knew she was acting in a stupid, childish manner, yet she seemed unable to control it. And she also knew that the reason for her pettiness was because she feared that Silas was disappointed in Doreen's refusal to help at the barbecue. Deep down it was Doreen he longed to see working beside him.

Bitter jealousy clawed at her, its sharp, painful talons filling her with an urge to scream with frustration and leaving her unable to think clearly. The fear that it might show on her face caused her to turn away from him and hasten towards the food hampers, and as she did so a shock revelation hit her with full force. *She was in love with him.* It was as Ling had said—she had only to look in her heart to see Silas.

The knowledge left her feeling shaken. It brought her to an abrupt halt on legs that felt suddenly weak, and several small gasps of dismay escaped her. And even as her mind tried to deny it, her basic honestly forced her to admit the truth. Yes—yes. . .*she loved him.*

But in the meantime the food awaited her attention, and the two rafts containing eighteen hungry men were riding the white foam, every minute drawing closer to the time when they must be fed. Silas needed her help at the barbecue and *she*—not Doreen—would be at his side to turn and serve the sizzling food. The thought caused her to hasten forward again, and moments later she was opening the food hampers.

The next few hours were spent in a daze while Lucy tried to disentangle the confusion in her bewildered mind. And as she worked beside Silas one question hammered to demand an answer—the question of how she could have lost control of her own emotions when she'd known that all he needed was time to sort out his own feelings for Doreen. And this would surely happen within a short period.

Nor could she have said what made her so positive about this assumption that had become a fixture in her head—unless it was the fact of Silas's previous near engagement to Doreen. Silas, she felt certain, was a man who would love only one woman, so it was natural that his affections would remain with Doreen. Yet there had been those kisses pressed upon her own lips—and what about the embraces that had held her so closely against him? The memory of them sent colour to her cheeks and a surge of excitement through her veins.

The excitement persisted as she worked beside Silas, making her acutely aware of his masculinity and of the vitality that seemed to ooze from every pore of his body. And at the same time she was only dimly conscious that the rafts had arrived, and that the men were changing into dry, warm clothing. It was time to place the food over the heat, and as she turned the sausages, bacon, tomatoes and potato patties, her hands became unsteady.

Lucy was also aware that Doreen's previous anger appeared to have vanished as she carried refilled plates back to the long table, where she chatted and laughed with the men and the two guides. On one occasion while having a plate refilled she beamed at Silas, then asked lightly, 'Am I making a satisfactory hostess for you, Silas darling?'

'You're doing fine,' he responded drily.

'This is nothing,' Doreen said gaily. 'Wait till you see me really getting into action as your hostess.'

'That should be interesting,' he grinned.

Doreen took a deep breath as she said in an urgent tone, 'I can't wait for you to make it *official*. Remember—we discussed it.'

'I recall that you brought up the suggestion and

positively hammered at it.' His face had become inscrutable.

Lucy waited anxiously, longing to hear him say that this would not happen, but the words failed to come. Her hands, already shaking, had become even less steady, causing the egg she was breaking to miss the hotplate and fall on to the red embers below. It sizzled, spluttered and smoked, sending an unpleasant odour into the air and completely overriding the previous appetising aroma of cooked sausages and bacon.

Doreen turned upon her with imperious authority. 'Watch what you're doing!' she snapped.

Lucy appealed to Silas, her face pathetic as she faltered, 'I'm sorry—it was an accident——'

'It was careless stupidity——' Doreen began, her voice raised.

'Shut up, Doreen,' Silas barked, his face contorted by a scowl. 'You are not the hostess yet.'

His words filled Lucy with relief, but she couldn't help wondering how long it would be before Doreen actually occupied that position. And what would Silas do about Stella? On her return, would she be casually dismissed from her job? No—Silas wouldn't treat Stella in that manner, Lucy decided in a burst of faith in the man she loved. But *that* was why he'd told Doreen she was not yet the hostess.

She also realised that—at the moment—Silas appeared to be annoyed with Doreen, but the reason for this escaped her. Could it be that he'd resented Doreen's attack on herself? No—that would be too much to expect, she decided with a pang of misery that made her blink as she turned over the food.

Or was he jealous? Had he observed Doreen's blatantly flirtatious manner towards the men of the rafting parties, to say nothing of her familiarity with the two guides? Her behaviour, Lucy suspected, was all part of an effort to arouse Silas's jealousy—but had the plan succeeded?

Watching Silas, the answer evaded her because his face remained expressionless, so she pushed the question away from her and got on with the job.

Eventually the men at the long table sat back in a happy state of having eaten and drunk as much as they could possibly hold. Doreen continued to hover about them, still chatting with forced brightness, but, instead of allowing herself to be drawn into their banter, Lucy made a start on preparing to leave. She began gathering plates and cutlery, then packed them into their hampers while the two guides dismantled the barbecue.

Silas began his routine of making sure that the shearers' quarters were being left in perfect order, and a short time later he spoke to Lucy. 'You'll drive home with us?' he queried, his dark eyes regarding her intently.

She did not reply at once, taking her time to empty the water from the snowdrop jar, then she glanced to where Doreen already occupied the front seat of the minibus. 'You mean—with you and Doreen?' she asked in a calm voice.

'Of course—and with others.'

Lucy took a deep breath. 'No, thank you, Silas. I came with Matt, so I'll return with him.' And then impulse caused her to be frank. 'In any case, I've had about as much as I can take from your dear friend for today—thank you very much.'

'Why do you let her get under your skin?' The abrupt question was laced with impatience.

'*Why*. . .? You need to ask. . .?' She fell silent, unable to speak openly—especially to this man—of the torment writhing within her.

He eyed her narrowly. 'What's happened to you? This morning you were your usual bright self, but now I suspect that something has really upset you—I mean apart from Doreen's bitchiness.'

Her eyes widened. 'You actually noticed it?'

'How could I miss it?' he snapped.

'You'd have to be obtuse to do so,' she flung at him, then changed the subject abruptly by saying, 'I really do believe that Ling is a wise man.'

'*Ling*? What the devil has he to do with this discussion?' His voice echoed exasperation.

'This morning I remarked upon the brightness of the day, but Ling warned that the clouds can gather. And they certainly did.' She paused, biting her lip while wondering if she should repeat other comments made by the Chinese. In fairness to the smooth running of the place, shouldn't Silas be warned of Ling's prediction of trouble?

He regarded her closely, his eyes again becoming narrowed as he spoke in a tone of command. 'Come on—out with it. What's going on behind those blue eyes, Miss Cornflower?'

She hesitated, then said carefully, 'Well—Ling happened to see Doreen clinging to your arm last evening when you were out in the moonlight.' It was difficult to keep the accusation from her voice, but she added calmly, 'It made him wonder how long she'll be staying here.'

'Why should it concern him?' Silas demanded crisply.

'Because he senses that she looks on him with disdain,' Lucy informed him. 'Her attitude towards him is sufficient to make him smell disruption.'

Silas frowned. 'What the hell does he mean by disruption?'

She gave a slight shrug. 'Do I have to spell it out, Silas? You haven't been on the receiving end of Doreen's barbs, but if they pierce Ling's skin to the extent of causing him to leave your service you can put a ring round the fact that there will be. . .definite disruption. If I were you I'd drop a quiet word in her ear before it's too late. Or do you imagine you can replace Ling with ease?' she finished drily.

'You seem to be taking a genuine interest in the place,' he commented with a touch of irony.

Goaded, she replied sharply, 'Haven't I done so from the moment of my arrival? Or is that another small point you've failed to notice?' she added bitterly.

Before he could reply, Doreen reached their side, her hands outstretched to clutch Silas's arm as she sent glances of suspicion from one to the other. 'Darling— we're ready and waiting to drive home,' she exclaimed. 'What on earth are you two talking about?'

'We were discussing the smooth running of the place,' he informed her nonchalantly.

'But shouldn't you be discussing that with *me*, rather than with *her*?' she protested, casting an icy glance over Lucy.

'Actually I intend to drop a word in your ear concerning the matter,' he said in a voice that now held a grim note.

Lucy stood watching as they walked to where his minibus stood parked. She saw him disengage his arm from Doreen's clinging fingers, but the action gave her little comfort. Then she sighed as she turned to where Matt's vehicle stood waiting. 'Never judge the day by the morning', Ling had said. How right he was.

Her face became set into a sober expression as she sat between Matt and one of the guides. Behind them the remainder of the rafting party sang popular songs during the homeward journey, but Lucy felt too miserable to join in.

Matt noticed her silence, and as he negotiated the bumps and pot-holes in the rough road he leaned towards her with a comment. 'I can't hear your voice singing along with the rest.'

She continued to stare ahead, wondering if he'd guessed her secret. Was her love for Silas written all over her face? She'd be wise to push him out of her mind—if this were at all possible—and before she made a complete idiot of herself. Then, realising that Matt required an answer, she said, 'I'm feeling a little tired, that's all.'

'Doreen wasn't much assistance to you?' he persisted shrewdly.

'None at all,' she retorted briefly. 'Nevertheless, she declares she's taking over as hostess—so obviously it's time for me to leave.'

'Don't do that,' Matt said in sudden alarm. 'That useless baggage would never make a good hostess—not in a thousand years.'

Lucy sighed and fell silent again. She had not exaggerated when she'd said she felt weary. Her emotional upsets were beginning to take their toll, and she knew that if she thought about the hopelessness of her love for Silas she'd begin to weep. And this she must guard against at all costs.

The journey home was slow because of the laden trailer being hauled behind them, but by the time they arrived she had herself under control. However, her feet dragged as she went towards the office, where she found Silas listening to the answering machine while Doreen recorded the messages.

Lucy waited until the task was finished, then sent a surprised glance towards the pad covered with Doreen's scribble. 'There seem to be more messages than usual,' she remarked.

Doreen giggled as a strange gleam of satisfaction leapt into her eyes. 'Oh, no—only three messages apart from a long one that concerns you,' she said with a hint of ill-concealed jubilation. 'Your aunt needs you at her side. Isn't that so, Silas?'

Lucy glanced to where the tall man stood at the window, his back turned towards them, apparently deep in thought, because he made no reply.

'Isn't that so, Silas?' Doreen repeated sharply. 'Lucy must go to her aunt—*at once.*'

'What is this?' Lucy demanded, a sudden apprehension gripping her as she stared from Doreen's smug face to Silas's back.

'It's on the machine. You can hear it for yourself if you doubt what I've written,' Doreen said, smiling broadly.

'Whatever it is, it seems to please you,' Lucy said, snatching the message pad from Doreen's hand, then found herself full of misgivings as she read the information directed to herself.

It had been sent by her aunt's neighbour who reported that Bertha had had an accident. She had been descending the stairs when she'd slipped and had fallen down numerous steps. Being a large woman, she'd landed heavily, badly hurting her left hip, her right knee and ankle. Fortunately she'd found herself within reach of the small hall table which held the telephone and had been able to ring her neighbour. She had been taken to Hastings Hospital and was now waiting for X-ray results. She'd like her niece to visit her as soon as possible.

Lucy was appalled by the thought of her aunt falling down the stairs and now lying in pain. Full of compassion, she exclaimed, 'Poor Aunt Bertha—I hope she's been given pain-killers——'

'Serve her right,' Doreen declared heartlessly. 'It's entirely her own fault——'

'Shut up, Doreen,' Silas snapped over his shoulder.

'It *is* her own fault,' Doreen persisted. 'She's getting no more than she deserves. If she'd left that house three years ago it wouldn't have happened. Silas—*darling*—can't you see what this means to *us*?' She clasped her hands, looking at him appealingly.

He turned slowly to stare at her. 'What are you talking about?'

Doreen's face became alight with sudden excitement, her eyes gleaming as she spoke rapidly. '*Can't you see*? This is the beginning of the end of her occupation of—

of *our house*. If her hip and knee and ankle are as badly damaged as I hope—I mean as they *could* be—she'll be unable to take herself up or down the stairs. I know there's a downstairs toilet, but all the bedrooms are upstairs. The house will no longer suit her.' Doreen began to laugh happily as these facts became confirmed in her mind.

Silas stared at her, his face expressionless. 'I had no idea you could be so damned cold-hearted, Doreen.'

Nor so stupid, Lucy thought privately. Couldn't she see that Silas was feeling disgusted with her lack of feeling towards an older woman who was now in a most awkward and painful situation?

Doreen flushed slightly, but ignored Silas's reprimand as she went on, 'I am not cold-hearted, Silas. I'm merely being practical when I say our plan is quite clear. We must find a ground-floor flat and have it ready for her to move into as soon as she comes out of hospital. All her personal belongings can be moved into it.'

'My aunt wouldn't like that,' Lucy protested. 'Nor do you know whether or not she'll be able to cope with the stairs.'

'Lucy's right,' Silas agreed. 'You're rushing along too quickly. In any case, Bertha must be allowed to choose whatever she wishes to take from the house.'

Doreen was aghast. 'Don't be silly, Silas. You'll not allow any of those beautiful antique pieces to be taken away by that old woman. You're forgetting they'll be *ours*——'

'And you're forgetting that she has the use of them during the period of her life,' he retorted crisply.

'Only while she remains in the house,' Doreen argued.

Lucy became exasperated. 'Are there any other arrangements you'd like to make for her—like where she's to be buried?' she demanded scathingly.

'When the time comes that will be a pleasure,' Doreen hissed in a vicious tone.

Lucy's tongue began to run out of control. 'What makes you so sure you'll be here to attend to it?' she almost shouted.

Doreen's chin rose as she declared with confidence, 'Of course I'll be with Silas. We'll be living in the home that is rightfully his. He'll sell this—this awful wilderness and return to his career of accountancy. He'll set up his own firm—isn't that so, darling?' She looked at him anxiously, obviously wondering if she'd gone a little too far.

She had. Silas barked at her in a fury. 'That's what you think, Doreen. You're making a mistake if you imagine you can manipulate my life like before. Those particular shackles have been torn off and tossed aside.'

'I—I'm afraid I was a little bit bossy in those days,' she admitted contritely. 'But I'm different now.'

'*A little bit*? You could have fooled me,' he snarled. 'You and Battling Bertha made a fine pair. You could've been her daughter.'

'Darling—can't you see I'm *different* now?' Doreen protested. 'Can't you see that I've *changed*?'

His brows rose. 'You have? I must be getting short-sighted—and maybe somewhat deaf. . .'

His words heartened Lucy to such an extent that uncontrollable giggles began to erupt from her until she became almost hysterical.

Doreen turned upon her in a fury. 'Isn't it time you got yourself down to the hospital to see that old bag in the bed? She demanded your presence *at once*—remember?'

The words recalled Lucy to her senses. 'Yes—perhaps you're right. I'll go during this evening's visiting hours.'

'That's ridiculous,' Silas said. 'She'll be under sedation. She won't even know you're there. Besides, you've had enough to contend with today,' he added with a side-glance at Doreen. 'I'll take you during tomorrow's visiting hours.'

Lucy blinked at him, scarcely able to believe her ears. 'You'll take me—to see Aunt Bertha? You'll actually come into the ward with me?' She watched him anxiously while waiting to hear that this would be too much to expect.

'Of course I'll come into the ward.'

'Oh, thank you, Silas. I'll be so grateful if you'll do that,' she said breathlessly.

'I'll come with you,' Doreen chimed in eagerly. 'I'd like to see the old—er—the *dear* soul again.'

Lucy felt herself go tense. She had no wish for Doreen to accompany them during this rare opportunity to be alone with Silas; then she sighed with relief as his next words rang like bells in her ears.

Speaking in a dry tone, he said, 'To be honest, Doreen, I doubt that this is an appropriate time for you to visit my stepmother—so Lucy and I shall go alone.'

The words were not like music to Doreen's ears. They caused her delicate brows to rise as she demanded indignantly, 'What do you mean? Why can't I come with you?'

He sent her a direct stare that was accompanied by the tightening of his jaw. 'Let's just say that I don't think Bertha would appreciate your particular brand of sympathy. It would be like kicking her when she's down—and I think she has enough to contend with at the moment.'

Doreen's eyes widened to express shocked dismay. 'Silas—are you saying you can't trust me to be *kind*?'

His grin was mirthless. 'Only when it suits you. You're forgetting I've known you since childhood, Doreen——' He broke off as Ling appeared at the door.

The Chinese held a piece of paper in his hand, and, sending Silas an apologetic look he said, "Scuse the interruption, boss. Tomorrow is Wednesday. My day off. Go to visit honourable mother in town. You like me to collect anything for you?"

'No, thank you, Ling. I'll be taking Lucy to see her honourable aunt.' He eyed the list in Ling's hand. 'Maybe the kitchen has needs? If so, we'll collect them.'

Ling grinned. 'Just a few items like the ever-disappearing sausages for the barbecue.' He advanced into the room to place his list on the desk near Doreen.

As he did so, she moved away with a look of distaste on her face. Nor was her action lost upon Ling, whose black eyes gleamed. 'The lady objects to me?' he asked softly. 'Or does she object to the coloured races in general?'

She had the grace to flush, but said nothing.

Silas glared at her with barely concealed fury. 'What the hell's the matter with you, Doreen?' he snarled.

Ling shrugged. 'It's OK, boss. The lady doesn't know the world has only two races—the intelligent and the stupid.' And with that subtle remark he left the room.

His departure was followed by a tense silence, until Silas turned bleak eyes upon Doreen. 'I can't understand what gets into you,' he rasped. 'You're continually bitchy towards Lucy, and now you're antagonistic towards Ling. For heaven's sake—*why?*'

'I'm sorry, Silas,' she mumbled, bringing forward her childish pout. 'I—I get this way when I'm unhappy.'

'Don't you mean when things are not going your way—and then you take it out on other people?' Silas's voice was like granite.

'It was because you're refusing to take me with you tomorrow. You'll be alone almost all day with *her.*' The last words were accompanied by a baleful glare at Lucy.

'And so you saw fit to vent your spleen on poor old Ling. What has he done to deserve your wrath?' Silas demanded. 'You'd be wise to tell me. I want this matter cleared up.'

Doreen looked down at her hands, then admitted reluctantly, 'If you must know—he told Jean he likes

Lucy, and that he hopes she will never leave this place. Can't you understand how it *riled* me?'

Silas drew a long breath. 'Can't *you* understand that he's the last person on the staff I want to see upset?'

Doreen's lip quivered as she looked at him reproachfully. 'You'd rather see *me* upset than *him*?'

'Definitely. He'd be really hard to replace. The mere thought of it gives me the horrors,' Silas admitted. 'And let me assure you of something else—anyone who interferes with the smooth running of this place can pack their bags and get down the road right away.'

Lucy looked at him in silence. And that also applies to me, she thought dolefully.

CHAPTER NINE

NEXT morning the atmosphere at breakfast did not lack strained moments. Silas had said he wished to leave for Hastings immediately after the meal, so Lucy came to the table ready to leave at a moment's notice. Her blue skirt and jacket made her eyes look like azure pools, and she had given herself extra time to wash her hair, which now framed her face with tendrils of spun gold.

Silas and Matt were at the table before her. They rose to their feet as she approached, both men casting glances of appreciation over her appearance. She smiled, feeling thankful she'd take so much trouble over her make-up— but who wouldn't when they were going out with Silas?

'Aye—you're a bonny lass,' Matt muttered gruffly.

Silas's eyes reflected something more than mere appreciation but he said nothing as he pulled out the chair for her to sit down.

And then Doreen entered the dining-room, walking carefully on her high spike heels. Her dark red suit, and the shoulder bag that swung carelessly, indicated that she also had a trip to town in view.

Again the men stood up, Matt attending to her chair. 'You're looking very smart this morning,' he said.

'Thank you.' She sent him a brief smile, then turned to beam at Silas. 'Don't I always look smart when I go out with you, darling?'

He looked at her grimly, then asked in a cool tone, 'Do you expect me to remember the clothes you wore three years ago?'

'Those three years don't exist, Silas. I've wiped them from my mind and I think you're about to do so as well.' She looked at him archly from beneath raised brows.

'You're wrong, Doreen,' he informed her calmly while a sombre note crept into his voice. 'Those three years were the best thing that could have happened to me. They gave me freedom. They showed me a new way of life. They taught me what I want and what I *don't* want.'

Particularly the latter, Lucy thought, looking at Doreen curiously. Why couldn't she see she was fighting a losing battle? Silas had made it plain that he didn't want women in his life, but she refused to accept that fact. Doreen, Lucy realised, was an expert self-deluder, who believed only what she wished to believe. Yesterday Silas had assured her he would not be taking her to town—yet here she was, smartly dressed and ready to accompany them.

Silas grinned as he spoke to Doreen. 'At least you'll look most elegant while acting as hostess in the office today. You'll give the place an air of high fashion.'

She thought for several moments, then twisted his words in an effort to pin him down to something definite. 'You're saying I can start in the office today as hostess— and that the job will be permanent? *Please*, Silas— promise it'll be permanent.'

'Certainly not,' he retorted curtly. 'That job belongs to Stella, for whom Lucy is merely standing in.'

'That's right,' Lucy said, unaware of the sadness in her eyes. 'As soon as Stella returns I'll be on my way.'

Doreen regarded her with a concentrated stare that attempted to pierce her mind. 'You really mean that?' she demanded with more force than necessary.

'Of course,' Lucy snapped. 'What else would you expect me to do?'

'You could have ideas of hanging round this place,' Doreen persisted relentlessly, glancing at Silas as she did so.

Lucy stared at her plate, expecting to hear Silas agree with her own statement that of course she'd be leaving— but he made no comment. Instead, he drained his coffee, then stood up. 'The car will be outside the front door in fifteen minutes,' he told Lucy, then left the room.

Later, she found herself in the front passenger seat of a comfortable grey Rover, and as the car negotiated the twists and turns of the mountainous road she stole side-glances at Silas's profile. He appeared to be deep in thought, frowning as he watched the highway ahead, and at last she felt she must say something to break the silence.

Forcing a smile, she turned to him and said, 'Thank you for taking me to see Aunt Bertha. It proves you're not as hard-hearted as I imagined. I know she's difficult, but at least you're showing you have some small feeling for her.'

He uttered a short laugh. 'It might surprise you to learn that I'm actually grateful to her. Yes—grateful on two accounts.'

She stared at him incredulously. 'You are? That's more of a shock than a surprise.' She continued to stare at him in silence, waiting for further explanation.

He went on, 'If it hadn't been for Bertha sticking to her guns over the question of the house, I'd have been married to Doreen by now—and that would have been a disaster.'

'You've really come to appreciate that fact?' It was difficult to keep the tremor from her voice.

'But you were right when you insisted that I must give myself the opportunity to learn my true feelings, although. . .' He fell silent.

She looked at him expectantly. 'Yes. . .? Although. . .?'

'I already knew them before she came.' His words held a ring of finality, as though the subject was closed.

But Lucy wanted to know more. 'Was she always so perpetually cross?' she queried.

'She was more subtle about it—but I'm afraid the fact

of finding you here has infuriated her into losing control of her temper. Her true colours have risen to the surface.'

'But she *knows* my period with you is only temporary.' Lucy held her breath while waiting for his answer. Again she was giving him the opportunity to ask her to lengthen the period—or to indicate in some way that he had no wish for her to leave. But the words remained unspoken, and again he appeared to have lapsed into deep thought.

Depressed, she leaned back in her seat, resting her head against the headrest while staring unseeingly at the hills and at the Esk River winding its way through the valley. And later she barely noticed the orchards where nectarine trees stood flushed with pink blossoms, and the upright branches of pear trees were thickly covered in white blooms. None of it registered, because she was fighting tears that were perilously near.

At last they reached Hastings, where Silas found his way to the suburban street of quality homes. He turned into the one occupied by his stepmother, switched off the motor, and for several moments they sat looking at the house whose drawn blinds and closed windows seemed to proclaim its emptiness.

'At least the garden is alive,' Lucy said. 'Just look at the brilliance of that yellow forsythia—and did you ever see such a border of anemones?'

'I like the magnolia and those camellias on the far side. I can remember my mother planting them. She was a keen gardener.'

She looked across the lawn to where the fallen pink camellia blooms lay like a mat beneath the dark green leaves. 'The place is full of memories for you,' she said in a voice that betrayed a depth of sympathy.

'You can say that again,' he admitted gruffly.

'Tell me about your mother.' The request came impulsively.

'She was sweet and kind. She was the opposite to Bertha. One might as well compare a soft grass path with a concrete walkway.' He paused, then gritted angrily, 'What the hell got into my father I'll never know.'

'It was probably the need for assistance,' Lucy said with sudden understanding. 'Despite her faults, Bertha is capable and a good housekeeper. Your father had to have somebody to take care of the house, as well as you and himself.'

'I suppose she did that,' he conceded grudgingly. 'But he didn't have to marry her.' The last words came as a snarl.

'Not all men are like yourself—completely averse to marriage,' she pointed out. Then, shying away from that particular subject, she said, 'Tell me more about your mother. What did she look like?' Her persistence, she admitted to herself, stemmed from a longing to learn more about his earlier life.

Unhesitatingly he said, 'She was tall and slim with dark hair and eyes. Actually, in appearance she was not unlike Doreen.'

'Well, that answers quite a lot,' Lucy said, drawing a deep breath to indicate she'd just seen the light.

'What do you mean?' he demanded sharply.

'It tells me why a man as strong as yourself would allow a woman like Doreen to dominate his life. She became a mother-figure. She looked like your mother whom you'd loved, but whom you'd lost—and while Doreen was near your mother seemed to be not so far away. Am I right?' She peeped at him to see the effect of her words.

'Yes, you're right,' he gritted angrily. 'But, for your information, Doreen is no longer reminding me of my mother. Over the last three years she's developed a hardness that Mother never had. But when I recall her attitude over this house I can't help wondering if that hardness has always been in her, and I was too dumb to see it.'

The twist of his mouth betrayed an inner fury, while his eyes blazed as he looked at her. His expression caused her to shrink back in her seat and exclaim with dismay, 'Silas—I feel you're becoming annoyed with me.'

'I'm infuriated with myself,' he gritted from behind clenched teeth, his scowl deepening.

'Then may we please drop this conversation?'

'You're the one who persisted with it,' he rasped. 'I dislike these confessions of stupidity being dragged from me. Now, then—shall we go inside?'

'Have you a key?'

'Of course I have a key. It's my house—remember?'

'Am I likely to forget?' she retorted as they left the car and went towards the front door.

Inside, the house was just as Bertha had left it when being carried away by ambulance. In the kitchen a few unwashed dishes remained on the table, and Lucy dealt with them at once by washing, wiping, and then putting them away. She then swept the kitchen floor, knowing her aunt would wish this to be done, and as she swished the few crumbs into the dustpan she heard Silas moving furniture in the dining-room.

Curiosity took her to the door. 'What on earth are you doing?' she felt compelled to ask while watching him stride across the room.

His reply came nonchalantly. 'I'm trying to decide upon the size of this room. I can't do it with chairs in the way.' He turned to pace the room lengthways.

She watched him for several moments, then looked about the large dining-room, trying to fathom the reason for his actions. At last, baffled, she said, 'I know it's not my concern, Silas—but would you please explain why this room has to be measured?'

He gave a sigh, then said patiently, 'Because it must be turned into a bedroom with en suite for Bertha. I doubt that she'll ever go upstairs again,' he added, going to the window and pushing aside the long red drapes.

'Wouldn't it be easier to install her in a flat?' Lucy suggested, her gaze moving from the mahogany table and matching red-seated chairs to the expensive oil paintings on the walls.

'Yes—but my father's will makes it clear he wished her to remain here, and, as you know, she has no desire to move.'

A frown creased Lucy's smooth forehead as she said, 'Even with a bedroom downstairs, I doubt that she should be living alone in this large house.'

'You're right. That's why I intend turning the upstairs area into a flat. I'll install a couple who will keep an eye on her and take care of the grounds.'

Bewildered, she followed him upstairs, then listened in a daze while he outlined his plan for converting the master bedroom into a lounge, and the smallest bedroom into a kitchenette. 'So this is why you were in a brown study for most of the journey into Hastings,' she said almost accusingly. 'You were planning all this?'

He grinned. 'You noticed I wasn't my usual chatty self? Once the idea took hold of me I couldn't rid myself of it.' Then, leading her into the generously sized guest-room that held two single beds, he said, 'This will become the main bedroom.'

She looked about the room, then said thoughtlessly, 'Doreen will be furious——'

The words were enough to make him explode with anger, and, turning swiftly to grip her shoulders, he shook her with force, glaring down into her face. 'What the hell has this to do with Doreen?' he barked. 'Haven't I given sufficient indication that I'll *never* marry her?'

Her teeth almost rattled from the onslaught as she stammered, 'I—I'm sorry—it—it's just a habit I've got into of—of coupling you together——'

'Then get out of it,' he snarled, still shaking her.

'*Stop it, Silas*—you're hurting me. Your hands are like steel claws.' The protest came as a wail.

His hands left her shoulders abruptly, his expression becoming suddenly shocked at the realisation of his actions. 'For Pete's sake!' he blurted out. 'I didn't mean to hurt you. Not for the world would I hurt you.'

'No. . .? You could've fooled me,' she lashed at him on a half-sob, her arms crossing her chest while her hands made an effort to massage the shoulder soreness caused by his gripping fingers. 'You don't know your own strength——'

'And you don't know how you frustrate me,' he retorted, tight-lipped, scowling at her.

She gaped at him. 'How can I possibly frustrate you? I do all I can to help you.'

His mouth twisted into a grim line as he admitted, 'You've been a marvel about the place, and I appreciate it. But that's all on the outside. It's what you do to my *inside* that gets me upset.'

Puzzled, she shook her head. 'I—I'm afraid I don't understand.'

'Believe me, I'd prefer you to remain in ignorance. Nor have I the slightest intention of subjecting you to a close examination of my emotions.'

'Are you saying they're in a restless state?' she asked carefully.

'They're like a tin of worms—wriggling and writhing.'

A feeling of gladness began to grow within her, manifesting itself in an exhilaration she found difficult to subdue. *He loved her*—she felt sure of it. He loved her, but wouldn't admit it. Those previous kisses had had meaning after all, and now he had only to utter those three little words that would send her up into the clouds. She looked at him pleadingly, trying to will him to say them.

He returned her gaze intently—but remained silent.

At last she sighed, realising she would have to wait

patiently, so she said, 'OK—so you're frustrated. But
frustration can be forgotten within moments, whereas
these bruises will give me ugly dark purple patches for
ages.'

'Bruises?' he queried doubtfully. 'Surely I couldn't
have been so rough? Let me see them and I'll kiss them
better.'

Her heart leapt at the words, but she said, 'No, thank
you—they can recover in their own good time.' Then
she stepped away from him, fearful of her own weakness
and afraid that if he kissed her she would dissolve into a
quivering jelly that would melt from sheer ecstasy.

But his arms reached to enfold her, drawing her
against his chest, where he held her closely for several
long moments. Then his fingers fumbled to unfasten the
small buttons of her suit jacket. The material was pushed
aside to reveal the red marks caused by the grip of his
fingers.

He stared at them aghast. 'Hell's teeth—did I do that?'
he muttered contritely. 'I had no idea. . .' His head bent
swiftly to kiss first one shoulder and then the other.

The touch of his lips on her skin sent tremors through
her as the blood began to dance in her veins, and, as his
mouth left her shoulder to trail an upward path, nuzzling
at vulnerable places on her neck and throat, her head
went back in submission. Her eyes closed as her lips
parted, then she gave herself up to the joy of feeling his
heart begin to thud.

The nuzzling continued as his lips found her own,
teasing and provoking her to yearn for more depth in the
caress, until suddenly he took possession of her mouth
in a forceful kiss that went on and on as though it would
last for ever.

His breathing became ragged, and as her arms wound
about his neck his hands slid down to grip her buttocks.
She arched against him, unable to control the flames of
desire leaping within her, then a gasp escaped her as he

swept her into his arms and carried her to the double bed in her aunt's room.

An instant later he was lying stretched beside her, resting on one elbow while his eyes burned with sombre intentness into her own. 'I want you, my darling,' he murmured huskily, his voice low and deep. 'But you know it only too well.'

His darling. She savoured the endearment—and yes, she knew he longed to make love. His arousal had made no secret of that fact. But first she must know that he loved her.

'You want me, too—it's useless to deny it,' he persisted, his voice still low. 'Inside you're glowing. Shall I fan the flames?'

Without waiting for a reply, he pushed aside the already unfastened fronts of her jacket, and then the shoulder-straps of her slip and bra. Her soft rounded breasts were revealed, peaked by erect nipples that stood up like rosebuds, and when his lips claimed them she was gripped by an aching pleasure that caused small sighs of ecstasy to betray her delight. Even so, her head remained clear enough for her to wonder when he would tell her he loved her.

Or was his delay caused by the fact that he was merely fond of her, and did not actually love her? Would this be just another experience for him—a satisfying of his sexual needs, to be forgotten within a short time? The thought made her feel cold, causing her to stir restlessly.

He sensed the subtle change in her, which was possibly betrayed by the firm manner in which she gripped the hand that moved towards her skirt waistband. 'You're afraid?' The question came quietly.

She nodded, scarcely daring to speak.

'It's because—it would be the first time?'

She nodded again. 'How—how did you know?'

'I sensed you were a virgin. Don't ask me how—but I

knew it without a shadow of a doubt. I suppose you want to keep it for your wedding night?'

'Yes—although heaven alone knows when that will be.' She waited, having given him the opening, but suggestions of love and marriage—or anything remotely related to them—still remained unspoken, and, sadly, she realised that he did not love her.

She made a move to button her jacket, but his hands forestalled the effort. 'Not until I've had more of their sweetness,' he pleaded, his thumb stroking one rosebud while his lips claimed the other.

Nor did she have the strength to be firm. Her longing for him was so intense that it filled her traitorous body with more waves of nerve-tingling sensations. Again she found herself responding to the fever of his passionate desire, and as her own need rose to meet it a small cry of yearning left her—a cry that was accompanied by a totally different cry that echoed from downstairs.

'Yoo-hoo. . .yoo-hoo. . .' a female voice called. 'Is anyone there?'

'Who the hell is that?' Silas gritted, leaping from the bed and straightening his shirt by tucking it into his trousers.

Lucy also left the bed in a hurry, fastening her jacket and then snatching up a comb that lay on the bedside table. She raked it through her hair as the voice came again.

'Yoo-hoo. . .yoo-hoo. . .it's Mrs Jensen—from next door. . .'

'She's the neighbour who phoned to tell us about Aunt Bertha,' Lucy whispered to Silas. 'She'll have noticed the car—and I think we left the front door open.'

'I'll talk to her,' Silas said. 'I'll arrange for her to collect Bertha's mail. Bills will have to be sent to me, and the newspaper will have to be cancelled,' he added casually as he made his way towards the stairs with complete composure.

Lucy stared from his retreating back to the indentations on the bedspread and pillow. He's forgotten those few minutes already, she thought resentfully while a state of depression began to grip her. But she was unable to see what she could do about it.

She then felt reluctant to go downstairs to face the man who had so recently been kissing her bare breasts, so she took extra time to straighten the bed where she had almost been willing to—no, *longing* to make love with Silas, she amended with a burst of mental honesty.

Eventually the time came when she couldn't delay going downstairs any longer, and when she reached the kitchen she discovered that the visitor had left, and that Silas was examining the contents of the fridge. 'It was Mrs Jensen from next door?' she queried, the needless question helping her to feel more normal.

'Yes. As you said, she saw the car and wondered who was here. She fears that Bertha's main problem will be her knee. Apparently it's badly damaged.' He regarded Lucy reflectively, then grinned as he said, 'It's just as well you didn't come downstairs in that tell-tale state.'

'Tell-tale? What do you mean?'

'Your jacket is wrongly buttoned. It's all skew-whiff.'

She looked down at the front fastenings, then her fingers shook as they fumbled to button the jacket correctly.

Watching her efforts, Silas said, 'Let me do it. I seem to recall being the culprit who caused this trouble.' And as he stood before her to correct the row of small buttons he asked, 'How would you like scrambled eggs for lunch?'

'*Scrambled eggs*. . .?' She looked at him bleakly, feeling more than a little hurt. While recalling their moments upstairs, he could speak of scrambled eggs. It was proof that what had meant so much to her meant little or nothing to him.

'If you'd prefer a meal in town——' he began.

'Of course not,' she said hastily. 'Scrambled eggs will

be fine. I'll find chives and parsley,' she added airily, making an effort to indicate that she also had forgotten the incident upstairs.

She went out into the garden, and when she returned he was preparing to cook toast and bacon. The kettle was put on for tea, and cutlery was laid on the kitchen table, which was covered by a cloth. Little was said during the meal, but as Lucy watched Silas make short work of the scrambled eggs she had cooked, she felt a quiet satisfaction.

A short time later he sat back and expressed his appreciation. 'That was a simple but really tasty meal. Ling couldn't have done better. I didn't know you could cook as well as. . .' He paused, looking at her thoughtfully.

She caught her breath. 'Yes. . .? As well as. . .?'

'Charm a man into insanity,' he concluded.

She looked at him in silence, wondering if insanity was being used as an excuse for their previous closeness. If so, she'd ignore the remark, and instead of delving further into the subject she said, 'You know perfectly well that the meal was a joint effort, because you cooked the bacon.'

'So I did. This domesticity is a nice change,' he declared. 'I'm enjoying it.'

'That's because there are no strings attached to it,' she commented airily, despite an underlying feeling of irritation.

He frowned. 'Strings? What do you mean?'

'Well, you're not tied down to a commitment of any sort,' she pointed out in a dry tone.

His frown deepened to a scowl. 'Are you suggesting that a commitment is beyond me?'

She forced a smile as she said artlessly, 'Oh, I'm not saying it's *beyond* you. I'm merely recalling what you yourself have indicated regarding your involvement with women. And that makes me wonder why you're not being more honest with Doreen.'

'*Honest!*' he barked, his eyes glittering with sudden

anger. 'Are you daring to suggest I'm being dishonest with Doreen?'

Lucy almost quailed beneath the onslaught of his wrath, but she persisted with her argument, mainly because she needed to have this point cleared in her own mind. Therefore she said, 'Less than an hour ago you stated that you will never marry Doreen. Right?'

'Right.'

'Then why don't you tell her so in plain language? Why do you allow her to continue with all this humbug of taking over as your hostess when you know she will never do so?'

'Because she would not believe me. She's brainwashed herself into believing otherwise,' he declared with conviction.

'Of course you know she's aiming to get you back into the city as an accountant?'

'Oh, yes—that has come through clearly enough.'

Lucy regarded him curiously. 'So what are you going to do about all these daydreams?'

'Nothing.'

'*Nothing*? Now that's what I mean about being dishonest. She should be told——'

He interrupted her impatiently. 'I shall do nothing for the simple reason that—knowing Doreen—it would be a waste of time and effort. She will believe the true situation only when she can see it for herself.'

'In the meantime it's possible you could lose Ling,' Lucy warned.

'Don't worry—I've had a word in his ear.'

She stood up and began to gather the plates, remarking as she did so, 'When I've washed these dishes it'll be time to leave for the hospital.'

Together they cleared the table, and as they moved about the kitchen Lucy thought of her aunt, and in doing so she remembered something that caused her to turn to Silas. 'You told me you were grateful to Aunt

Bertha on two accounts,' she reminded him. 'The first was for saving you from a fate worse than death with Doreen—but what was the second reason?'

His silence following the question made her wonder if it was something he had no wish to divulge, but at last he said with simple sincerity, 'She sent you to me.'

'You mean you're grateful to her for sending someone with an ulterior motive?'

'At least you helped me out when Stella became ill.'

And therein lay the extent of his gratitude, she realised with a feeling of despondency, but to disguise her feelings she added brightly, 'When we're at the hospital we must visit Stella.'

'We'll do that,' he agreed gravely.

The bell to announce the visiting hour had already been rung by the time they reached the hospital, and, after walking along corridors in the company of numerous people who carried flowers and parcels, they found themselves in a ward filled with beds and patients. The air hung with an antiseptic aroma peculiar to hospitals, and as she passed elderly sick people Lucy suddenly felt very young and healthy.

Silas spoke to the sister in charge of the ward, who told him a little about Bertha's injuries. Her hip had suffered a bruise that would heal, but it was feared that her knee and ankle could give trouble—possibly for the rest of her life.

'How will she be on stairs?' Silas queried.

'She won't be on stairs—not if she can help it,' the sister retorted briefly.

They found Bertha in a slightly drowsy state that signified drugs were keeping severe pain at bay, while a long bulge beneath the bedclothes indicated that her leg was in a plaster cast. Nevertheless, she was sufficiently alert to give vent to her usual state of ill-humour.

Glaring from one to the other as they stood on either

side of the bed, she said crossly to Lucy, 'So you've brought him to see me at last. I must say you've taken long enough to do so.'

Lucy made an effort to placate her. 'No, Aunt—Silas has brought *me* to see *you*.'

Bertha turned reproachful eyes to Silas. 'It seems I have to fall down the stairs before you'll deign to visit me,' she declared in an aggrieved tone that held a touch of vinegar.

His lips twisted into a mirthless grin. 'Dear Bertha— I see you're still your same sweet and gracious self,' he commented on a sardonic note.

She sniffed as her voice rose slightly. 'You've won, haven't you? You and that woman—*that Doreen*——'

Silas's brows rose. 'Is that a fact? In what way have we won?'

'You've got me out of the house at last,' Bertha whimpered. 'I'll have to move out while you and she move in. It's the *stairs*, can't you understand?'

Lucy took her aunt's hand and patted it. 'They won't do that, Aunt,' she assured her gently. 'Silas intends turning the house into two flats so that you can live downstairs.'

Bertha's eyes widened as they turned to him. 'Is this true? You'd really do this for me?'

Silas's face and voice were expressionless as he said, 'It's what my father would expect me to do.'

Bertha's lip quivered. '*Dear* boy—you're so like your father. Oh, how I miss him.' She reached for a tissue to dab at the moisture welling in her eyes.

They did not stay long, because her drowsiness began to increase, and a short time later they left to go in search of Women's Surgical, where Stella greeted them with pleased surprise.

'I'll be home in a few days,' she told them happily. 'And then you'll be able to go to *your* home,' she added to Lucy.

Silas said firmly, 'I shall not allow you to rush into the office the moment you return. You'll need a period of convalescence. I'm sure Lucy will agree to stay until you're feeling stronger. Isn't that so?' He raised a dark brow in her direction.

Lucy looked at him wonderingly. Was this his way of prolonging her stay without telling her he wanted her to be there? But of course—it was the barbecue where her presence was so necessary.

Stella sent her a sympathetic look. 'I suppose you've had enough of Wilder's Wilderness?'

'Not at all,' Lucy replied, knowing she could never have enough of the place which was a strange mixture of excitement on the river and tranquillity in the bush. And apart from these two activities she would like to indulge in more horse-riding.

'It's Wilder himself who has got under her skin,' Silas commented drily. 'Wilder—and his odd ways with women.'

'Now what would he mean by that remark?' Stella queried lightly, looking at Lucy with sudden interest.

'Heaven alone knows,' Lucy returned in an equally light tone. Had Silas realised she'd fallen in love with him? Were there times when it was written all over her face? The mere thought sent a flush to her cheeks.

Stella gave a teasing laugh as she said, 'Everyone at the Wilderness knows that he runs away from women— but one day he'll be caught. He'll meet his match.'

'I doubt it,' Lucy said with as much calm as she could muster, trying to ignore the surge of misery growing within her. Of course Silas knew she was in love with him, she decided, feeling acutely embarrassed. No doubt it amused him, but although he didn't laugh outright he took this way of telling her she could forget it. This was his way of reminding her that he intended to remain free.

CHAPTER TEN

SILAS was not slow to move, Lucy realised.

When they left the hospital he studied Ling's list, and within a short time the purchases had been made, the sausages being stored in a coolbox to keep them cool. He then drove to the office of a friend who was an architect, and within minutes had persuaded him to come and examine the job to be done on the house. It was a matter of urgency, he assured the man, who was introduced to Lucy as Peter Bush.

When they returned to the house Silas and Peter Bush walked from room to room with Lucy hovering in the background. The architect assured Silas that the task would not be too difficult because the present plumbing arrangements could be incorporated in the new upstairs kitchen and the downstairs en suite. He made notes and said that if he had a key to the house he'd be able to plan what was needed in a shorter time. Silas then gave him his key, and a promise was made to send a copy of the plan as soon as possible.

Little was said on the homeward journey. Silas appeared to be deep in thought, while Lucy sat wrapped in a gloom which sent her down a dark tunnel to the depths of depression. Stella would be home soon, she realised, and, despite her period of convalescence, Lucy's own days at Wilder's Wilderness were numbered. She'd have no further excuse to remain, and even her reason for going there had now been achieved. Silas had visited his stepmother, even if the circumstances had left much to be desired.

Lucy contemplated her future, which seemed to stretch before her in a pattern of bleakness, especially where her social life was concerned. Most of her girl-friends lived with the hopes and aims of finding a husband among a crowd of men whose principal interests lay in rugby, racing and beer, and, of course, in getting a girl into bed if possible.

Among the crowd there was nobody like Silas. Nobody with his integrity and substance—and again she marvelled that he would go to the extent of altering his house to enable his anything-but-lovable stepmother to live in it. And this costly project was being undertaken through a strong sense of duty to what he believed his father would have wished him to do.

Nor did his consideration for Stella escape Lucy's ponderings—nor his thoughtfulness in allowing Bill to have time off, which enabled him to be near his wife during her period in hospital. It all added up to the fact that below Silas's cool exterior there was warmth and compassion for others.

Her thoughts turned to Doreen. Had she discovered insincerity and instability among Australian men? Was this the reason for her return to Silas? Although she *had* mentioned a man named Clive. It had been a slip on Doreen's part, Lucy recalled as she found herself wondering what the situation had been with Clive.

'You're very silent,' Silas said at last.

'I was thinking about Doreen,' Lucy said with truth. 'I hope I'm not around when she learns about the alterations to the house. She'll be livid.'

'She'll not learn about them unless you tell her. I'd advise you to maintain a dead silence on the subject,' he said in a voice that was full of warning.

Lucy had already decided that this would be the wisest course for her to take. After all, there was no need for Doreen to learn of what was about to happen to the house. If Silas had no intention of marrying her, the house was no longer her concern. To change the subject she said, 'I'm sure Stella will be glad to be home again.'

'Just as you'll be glad to return to your home again,' he remarked drily.

She stared straight ahead. 'Have I indicated in any way that I'm itching to go home?'

'No—but there have been times when I've suspected you'd like to pack your bag and jump into that red Toyota.'

'But the reason has escaped you?' she queried sweetly, thinking of Doreen.

For several moments he made no reply, then he sent her an enquiring glance as he said, 'May I ask a favour?'

'Of course.' She glanced at him in quick surprise, wondering what sort of favour he could possibly have in mind.

'Well—I'd be grateful if you'd stay until after the Women's Institute bush walk is over. Is that too much to ask?'

Nothing was too much to ask if it prolonged her stay, she thought wistfully, so she smiled as she said, 'Considering that I was the culprit who booked them in on Ling's day off, it's the least I can do.' Then she added with sudden firmness, 'But after that I shall go home. I shall phone Mother this evening and tell her about Aunt Bertha. . .and that I'll be home on—on Thursday week.'

'Thank you—and I mean that. What's more, I intend to say it properly,' he declared, reducing speed to turn into a parking area that lay a few yards ahead. He then unclipped his seatbelt and turned towards her, his arms enfolding her as he murmured, 'You are a dear girl. I'm thankful you'll stay the extra time.'

She unfastened her own belt, and as her arms wound about his neck their lips met in a long kiss. Nor were they concerned by drivers who tooted horns as they sped past. They had floated into a dream world of their own, and Lucy's pulses were racing as she waited to be told he loved her.

Desperately, she waited to hear the words. Have

patience—have patience, she told herself while his lips trailed a line from her mouth to her ear, where they nibbled her lobe. Vulnerable places on her neck and throat were kissed before his lips found their way to her breast, where her nipples had again firmed into rosebuds.

At last he raised his head to regard her seriously. 'You were ready to make love this morning,' he said quietly. 'If the lady from next door hadn't come with her yoo-hooing you'd be a different person now.'

Lucy's colour rose as memory of lying on the bed beside him sent a wave of desire through her, but she pushed the yearning away, making an effort to speak calmly. 'I thought you'd forgotten about this morning,' she said in a small voice.

'You did?' He sounded pained. 'How *could* I forget about this morning? What gave you that impression?'

'Your casual attitude. It seemed as if you'd swept those moments from your mind—at least, you made me feel you were doing your best to forget them.' Her voice held a sadness she was unable to disguise.

Silas spoke with infinite patience. 'It didn't occur to you that I might have a lot on my mind? There was Ling's list to be purchased from the wholesale stores. . . alterations to the house to be considered. . .an architect to pin down while I was in town and had the opportunity to do so——'

'I—I suppose I was being unreasonable,' she said, feeling slightly relieved. *Of course* he'd had a lot on his mind.

'And there was Bertha with the stuffing knocked out of her. Would you believe that the sight of her in that condition made me feel differently about her? All my previous resentment seemed to vanish.'

'I'm glad of that,' she said softly.

'But as for forgetting about this morning's little episode. . .personally, I suspect that you'll be the first to do so.'

'You do? What makes you so sure about that?'

'The fact that you'll be among your old friends, who will all clamour to know where you've been.' He paused, his dark eyes resting on her face and seeming to take in every detail, committing them to memory. 'I shall miss you,' he muttered in a low voice. 'In fact, I don't know how I'll get on without you.'

The unexpected admission made her heart leap, causing her to turn and look at him with eyes that were bright with hope. But he remained silent, and, despondently, she turned away again, realising that there would be no words of love coming from this man, who now held her heart in the palm of his hand.

'I said I'll miss you,' he repeated, his deep voice still low. 'Doesn't it mean anything to you?'

Oh, yes, he'd miss her, she thought—especially at the barbecue. Aloud she answered his question. 'Of course it means something to me—but I know you'll survive. You're an expert at surviving without being close to a woman. You've had three years of practice. In any case—you'll have Doreen.'

'Must you continue to throw her at me?' he gritted in sudden anger. Then he turned from her abruptly, fastened his seatbelt, and switched on the ignition key. The next instant the car shot forward to leave the parking area and regain the highway.

Lucy gnawed her lower lip while she sat cursing her stupidity in bringing up Doreen's name. She knew they'd been on the verge of drawing at least a little closer to each other, yet she had been the one to ruin the opportunity. Nor was she surprised when Silas lapsed into silence during the remainder of the journey, and when they reached home she hastened to her room, where tears of frustration rolled down her cheeks.

* * *

Nor did her depression disappear next morning when Doreen came to the breakfast table, dressed in pale fawn jodhpurs. She posed languidly before Silas, smoothing her hips provocatively as she spoke with coyness, 'Remember my old joddies, darling? As you can see, they still fit me.'

He ran an eye over her slim figure. 'So you've decided to give them an airing?'

She flicked a triumphant glance over Lucy. 'Yes. I noticed there are horse treks arranged for the next three days. I've decided to come with you—as your hostess. Darling, please select a good mount for me. Nothing too mettlesome, because I haven't ridden for more than three years.'

Matt bent a kindly glance upon Lucy. 'When shall you be riding again, lass?'

But Lucy felt unable to speak. She merely shook her head while jealousy gnawed at her. The vision of Doreen, head erect, and full of confidence as she rode beside Silas, was all too clear. In comparison, she herself would look little better than a sack of potatoes on horseback.

Despite her depression she occupied herself with office tasks, and, although there were times when she dabbed at a tear, she reminded herself that she must prepare for the time when she would never see Silas again. So, when the riding party of teenage girls returned for a late lunch, Lucy forced herself to present time with a brightly smiling face.

Dejection was again with her next morning, pressing heavily to remind her that she would face another day of visualising Doreen riding knee to knee beside Silas. She dressed slowly, feeling reluctant to go to the breakfast table, and she was almost ready to leave the room when she was startled by the sound of a light tap on the bedroom door. It was followed by Silas's voice.

'Lucy—are you in there?'

'Yes—I'm here.' She opened the door and was surprised to find him holding the jodhpurs she had worn during her first ride.

'You'll put these on,' he said, passing them to her.

She stared at the riding trousers, feeling slightly bewildered. 'But—isn't Doreen——?' she began.

'Don't argue. Just get yourself ready to ride.' And with that he strode along the passage.

When she reached the breakfast table, Silas, Matt and Doreen were already seated at it. The latter was again dressed in readiness to mount a horse, but the sight of Lucy brought a flash of indignation to her eyes. 'Where do you think you're going?' she demanded angrily. 'Or is this a new form of office attire?'

Lucy ignored her, deciding that Silas could deal with this little scene, particularly as he was the cause of it.

Nor did he hesitate to acquaint Doreen with the situation, and, speaking quietly, but with a determined edge to his voice, he said, 'Today is Lucy's turn to come riding. You had your turn yesterday—and today is your turn in the office. Is it understood?'

Doreen's jaw sagged slightly, then she muttered in a sulky manner, 'I suppose so——'

'I should jolly well think so,' Matt put in, eyeing her sternly.

She glared at him, but decided to remain silent.

A short time later, while riding beside Silas, Lucy felt as if she were in a dream. She made an effort to recall all he had told her during the previous ride, and paid attention to the way she sat, as well as to the positions of her hands, elbows, knees and heels.

As they moved along the route she became aware of birds singing in the trees, and of sheep grazing peacefully in the fields. The distant mountain ranges made her think of giants sleeping beneath blue blankets, but most of all she was vitally conscious of Silas, who guided the party of young women over hills, down valleys and along a track beside the bush.

Drawing to her side, he said, 'You're doing well. I can see you're remembering my instructions.'

'Does that mean you've been watching me?' she asked, flushing beneath his praise.

'Of course I've been watching you. Each member of the party comes in for my scrutiny,' he informed her.

'Oh.' She tried to hide her disappointment. What a fool she was, imagining he would have singled her out. However, his next words dispelled some of her gloom.

'Those jodhpurs fit you very well. They could have been tailored for you. I'll put them away for when you come back.' The last words came casually.

She shot a rapid glance of enquiry at him. 'Come back? Are you saying you think I'll return?'

'Probably sooner than you think, Miss Cornflower.'

She looked away into the distance. 'What makes you so sure of it?'

He avoided her question by asking another. 'Are you hinting you have no wish to set eyes on this place again?'

'Of course not—I love the place. . .' She bit off further words, feeling irritated with herself for having made that admission.

'You do? Oh. . .well. . .in that case. . .' He paused, frowning while staring ahead at some of the other riders, then he said, 'Excuse me—I must stop them from taking the wrong track.' Then he left her side, cantering to where some of the party needed guidance in the right direction.

Hopefully, she waited for him to return to her side, but when he failed to do so she realised that whatever he had been about to say would be left unsaid. And also that whatever she felt about his property was of little interest to him.

Few words passed between them during the remainder of the horse trek, and even during lunch Silas appeared to be more silent than usual, a fact which drew a comment from Matt.

'You're very quiet,' the older man remarked. 'Why so thoughtful?'

Silas grinned at him. 'I'm doing a mental count of the number of wool packs we have in the shed. Shearing is coming up and we need to have plenty on hand.' He then finished his lunch and left the table.

Watching through the window, Lucy saw him make his way towards the wool shed, his strides long, as though he wished to get there in a hurry. She was then assailed by the oddest feeling that he was avoiding any prospect of the continuation of the conversation begun during the horse trek.

What had been the rest of that unfinished sentence? she wondered. And how could he be so sure she'd return? Possibly it was because most people who visited Wilder's Wilderness expressed the wish to return. And after all— as far as Silas was concerned—wasn't she just one of the rest of the crowd?

Next morning Doreen arrived at the breakfast table, her attire indicating she was ready to join the horse trek. 'May I ride with you this morning, Silas darling?' she cooed in honeyed tones.

'You may ride—but not with me,' he informed her blandly. 'Bill Martin is bringing Stella home this morning. He'll take the horse treks from today, because it's really his job. As for me—I'll be busy in the office. I've a pile of farm accounts to check with Lucy.'

'I could help,' Doreen put in eagerly.

'Thank you—but it won't be necessary. Besides, you'll be out riding—and busy playing at being hostess,' he added with a laugh.

Matt put in a warning. 'Just let Bill hear you say you're the hostess and he'll have your ears for horse blinkers. That's his wife's job, as you are well aware.'

Doreen took umbrage. Glaring at Matt, she snapped,

'How *dare* you say my ears could be used for *horse blinkers*? I consider my ears to be *small*—and I think you're very rude.' And with that final remark she sprang to her feet and left the room.

'Now you've upset her,' Silas remarked, watching Doreen's retreating back.

Matt was unrepentant. 'It's high time somebody did—and how you tolerate her I'll never know. Personally, I'd tell her to get herself down the road in double-quick time.'

Silas shook his head. 'But you don't know Doreen. If I do it that way she'll either refuse to go, or, if she *does* go, she'll be back within a short time.' He paused thoughtfully, then added, 'If I have patience the situation will resolve itself.'

'How can you be sure?' Matt asked doubtfully.

'I'm not. It's just a feeling I have,' Silas admitted.

Lucy was only half listening to their conversation, the main thought in her own mind being that Stella would be home today. And while she was pleased for Stella to be out of hospital and in more comfortable surroundings, she knew it heralded the beginning of the end of her own sojourn at Wilder's Wilderness.

Silas, she realised, also recognised this fact, and that was why he'd suddenly become conscious of the farm accounts. Recently, he'd left them very much in her hands, but now, with her own departure looming, he'd decided it was necessary to go through everything with her. Nor need she expect anything more than a strictly business afternoon, she warned herself.

But, despite this assumption, they sat at the desk so closely that their bodies were almost touching, and there were times when his arm encircled her shoulders while he leaned forward to check additions on the electronic calculator. At such moments it was difficult to remain calm, but she forced herself to concentrate on the figures until eventually the task was finished.

Silas then sat back with a satisfied air, his eyes holding admiration. 'You're very good—you'd be an asset to any man's business.'

Resentment flashed into her eyes as she said in a pained voice, 'If ever the time *does* come, I hope I'll be wanted for more than my ability with figures.'

'I think you can count on it, Cornflower,' he said softly, then changed the subject by saying, 'I haven't shown you what came in the mail today.'

'Do you mean that mailing tube with the architect's name on it? It can only be the plans for the house alterations,' she guessed.

He took the tube from a drawer, and when the desktop had been cleared of papers the plans were spread open. Together they studied the downstairs bedroom with its en suite, and then the upstairs kitchen with its cupboards, sink unit and plumbing details.

'I'll leave the plans on the desk,' he said, rolling them and replacing them in the tube. 'If you think of anything that can be added you can give them further study.'

She hesitated, then suggested tentatively, 'We could show them to Aunt. After all, she's the one who will live there—and it might help her to feel better.'

'OK—we'll go and see her again.'

She breathed a sigh of relief. 'Thank you, Silas.'

And then came the first Wednesday in October—the day of the Woman's Institute bush walk. If it had been pouring with rain the walk would have been cancelled, and that would have been more in keeping with Lucy's mood, which was one of deep depression.

Today she didn't even glance at the cloudless blue sky. She saw nothing of the pale green clusters of new leaves adorning the elm trees, nor did she see the arum lilies glowing with white purity beneath them. She knew only that today was the last she'd spend at Wilder's Wilderness, and the knowledge caused her to be wrapped in misery. Only with difficulty was she able to hold back the tears, forcing herself to smile.

The coach arrived early in the afternoon, and as it approached the front entrance Silas went out to meet it. Doreen followed him closely, and, as the driver opened the door for Silas to enter, Doreen slipped in behind him.

'Huh—would you look at that,' Jean said from the doorway. 'A fat lot of help we can expect from *her*.'

'We don't need it,' Lucy assured her as the coach continued along the road towards the bush. She was feeling thoroughly angry, but she hid it from Jean as she went on, 'Ling has shown us where the cakes, sandwiches and asparagus rolls are in the deep-freeze, and we know exactly when to defrost them in the microwave ovens—so why should we worry about Doreen?'

'Shall I ask Mum to help us?' Jean queried. 'She's longing to get to work again. After all, it's now only afternoon tea, instead of lunch as we at first thought it would be.'

'Certainly not,' Lucy said sharply. 'She was up for the entire morning, and this afternoon she must rest. It takes ages to get over operations.' Then, turning towards the kitchen, she said, 'We'd better make sure the urns are full of water.'

They went into Ling's spotless domain, where they attended to setting out cups and saucers, jugs of milk and bowls of sugar on the bench beside the wide servery. And, as they worked, Lucy's imagination carried her away to the bush, causing her to torture herself with thoughts of Doreen's fingers sliding down Silas's arm to clasp his hand. Despite everything he'd said to the contrary, he *might* retain tender feelings for Doreen, and the fear of this caused jealousy to writhe and twist in Lucy's mind until her face became pale and her hands shook.

Her state of agitation conveyed itself to Jean, who

looked at her with concern. 'You're worrying too much about this job,' she said. 'It's nothing more than a crowd of women having a cup of tea. And there's plenty of time because the moment they return they'll all line up at the toilets.'

'Yes—of course you're right. I'm being an idiot,' she said, glad that Jean could find an excuse for her stupidity. And it was enough to make Lucy pull herself together. A fine fool she'd look if Silas returned and found her in a state of emotional upset. And if it had been obvious to Jean then Silas would notice it in two seconds or less. Perhaps he'd guess that her trouble was *jealousy*.

By the time the coach returned she had herself under control. The large teapots were filled from the boiling urns, and, thanks to the microwaves, the food tasted as if it had been freshly made. She flushed as she became conscious of Silas watching her pour the tea, but suddenly she noticed him scowl as his attention was caught by Doreen's voice, which could be clearly heard.

Doreen, it seemed, was wafting among the women, attending to refills of tea, and chatting loudly about her duties as hostess in a place such as Wilder's Wilderness. And, as Silas stood listening to her, Lucy noticed his jaw tighten in anger.

A short time later, when it was almost time to board the coach, the Institute's president called for silence. She then thanked Silas for his informative talk on New Zealand's native trees and birds, and declared that the afternoon tea had been delicious. Her words were followed by applause to indicate that everyone agreed.

In response Silas said, 'Thank you, ladies. We aim to please.' He then requested Lucy and Jean to come from the kitchen, and, standing between them, he placed an arm round their shoulders as he said, 'This is Lucy and Jean, who have attended to your refreshments on behalf of Stella, my hostess, who is indisposed. Jean is Stella's daughter, and Lucy has been acting as hostess in her place.'

His words were followed by a silence as the women turned with one accord to stare at Doreen. She went crimson, then left the room, her exit being followed by a burble of chatter as the women expressed their surprise.

Lucy turned to Silas. 'Was it necessary to tell them?' she asked in a low voice. 'Doreen will be hopping mad.'

He sent her a bleak look. 'Yes, it was necessary. Her lies about being hostess had to be stopped. They'd have reached Stella's ears and I'll not tolerate her being upset.'

When the time came for the women to take their seats in the coach, Silas, Lucy and Jean stood to wave farewell. But of Doreen there was no sign—at least not until they went inside and she emerged from her bedroom, where she had been weeping.

She flung herself upon Silas, grasping his arms as she gazed up into his face, and despite the presence of Lucy and Jean she wailed contritely, 'Silas, *darling*—I'm so sorry. I really did get a bit beyond myself. It was just that I was *longing* to be your hostess.'

'Is that a fact? It's a pity you didn't think about it more carefully three years ago—or maybe it's just as well,' he mocked.

Her anger surfaced. 'You know whose fault *that* was— *her* blasted aunt.' She sent a baleful glare towards Lucy, then turned to Silas again. 'Darling, I won't mention the word hostess again—ever—I promise.'

'See that you keep it,' he instructed briefly.

'Please stop being angry with me,' Doreen pleaded in a wheedling tone, rubbing her hand along his arm.

The action infuriated Lucy, who felt she'd heard and seen enough of Doreen's tactics. She sent Jean a quick glance as she said, 'We'll put those dishes through the machine.' Then, without looking at Silas, she made her way along the passage, closely followed by the younger girl.

When they reached the kitchen Lucy collected the cups and saucers while Jean rinsed the crumbs off them and stacked them in the dishwasher. Benches were wiped, floors were swept, and within a short time Ling's kitchen had been restored to the pristine condition in which they had found it.

They were on the verge of finishing when Silas came to the kitchen. He stood at the doorway regarding the room with approval before he said, 'Thank you, girls—you've done an excellent job.'

Jean laughed, then said airily, 'We couldn't have managed without *Doreen's help*.'

The mere mention of Doreen's name was sufficient to stir the frustration simmering in Lucy's mind, and this, coupled with jealousy that refused to be submerged, forced her to say, 'Your friend is not in need of further consolation after such trauma?'

He sent her a bleak look. 'I wouldn't know,' he responded in a cool voice. 'At the moment she's in the office, speaking on the phone to her mother, who had an urgent message of some sort.'

Lucy felt a sudden apprehension. 'In the office—where the phone is on the desk? Aren't the plans for the alterations also on the desk? They'll be right under her nose——'

Her words were interrupted by Doreen sweeping into the room with the plans in her hand. Her face was flushed, her eyes glittered, and her voice shook as she hissed at Silas, '*What is this?*'

He looked at the unrolled papers, then drawled nonchalantly, 'As you've already studied them, I presume you'll know exactly what they are.'

She shook the papers as though they were two rag dusters. 'They appear to be plans for turning *our house* into two flats.'

'Stop brainwashing yourself, Doreen. It's *my* house—not *our* house.' His jaw had tightened and his voice had become hard.

'But Silas, darling—I've come for us to take up where we left off——'

'So you said—but that will never happen, Doreen, and the sooner you wake up to that fact, the better it'll be for youself.'

'You don't mean that, Silas,' she wailed. 'I know you don't meant it. And it's sacrilege to even *think* of altering that lovely home.' She took a deep breath as her agitation mounted. 'I suppose it's to enable blasted Bertha to remain in it—just when you have the opportunity to get her out. Silas—*you must be mad.*' The last words were shrieked at him as Doreen worked herself into a frenzy of rage which caused her to tremble violently.

'You needn't bother to put on that act with me,' Silas rasped at her. 'It'll get you nowhere.'

But it wasn't an act. Doreen was really going berserk while continuing to shout at Silas. 'That's *our house*,' she ranted. 'I won't have it altered—do you hear?' She then tried to tear the plans in half, but the paper was of a strong variety.

Silas snatched them from her shaking hands. 'Control yourself, you silly witch,' he barked at her.

His words infuriated her even further. 'It's *her* fault,' she shrieked wildly, spinning round to spit hatred at Lucy. '*She's* persuaded you to do this mad thing, but she won't get away with it—not if I have any say in the matter. . .' Then, before anyone could stop her, Doreen rushed across the kitchen to slap Lucy's face and pound viciously at her head with closed fists.

Lucy screamed and tried to protect her head and face with her arms while Silas sprang across the room and dragged Doreen from her. His arms went about Lucy, holding her against him, then he spoke to Jean. 'This is not your scene, Jean. Please go and keep an eye on the office.'

Jean fled from the room.

Silas turned to where Doreen leaned in a crouched position against the bench. 'For your information, Lucy and I are to be married—as soon as possible.' His arms tightened about her. 'At least—that's if she'll have me.'

Doreen's laugh bordered upon hysteria. 'You mean you're only just asking her? I don't believe this nonsense.'

Lucy didn't believe it either. It was just a spur-of-the-moment plan to rid himself of Doreen, she decided, but, even so, her arms became firmer as they clung to him. Then, realising that he was looking down into her face while waiting for her to say something, she nodded her head as she said, 'A fine proposal this is, I must say.' To herself she added silently, But better than no proposal at all. That's if he means it, of course—which I doubt.

Above her head Silas murmured, 'I'll admit I've been slow—but we'll make up for it later, my dearest.'

She was still full of doubt as she said, 'You haven't been slow—you've just been too busy weaving a net round yourself to keep the female species out of your life.'

'I must have left a hole somewhere, because one has slipped through —straight into my heart.'

There was a burst of sobbing from Doreen. 'I loathe and detest you both,' she panted venomously. 'You make me want to *throw up*.'

'Then take yourself outside,' Silas ordered heartlessly. 'I'll not have Ling's floor in a mess.'

But before Doreen could make a retort Jean returned to the kitchen and, standing at the doorway, she looked from Doreen to Silas. 'Excuse me, boss,' she said. 'There's a man at the reception desk. He says he's come to find Doreen.'

Doreen was suddenly very still, almost as if she were

unable to move. 'Wh—what does he look like?' she quavered nervously.

The question was answered almost immediately because the man, who had followed Jean along the passage, now pushed past her and entered the kitchen. He appeared to be in his late thirties. His reddish hair was receding at the temples and his grey eyes rested upon Doreen with obvious relief. 'Ah, there you are, baby—I've come to fetch you home. That's if you'll come.' His voice held an unmistakable Australian accent.

'Oh, Clive—of course I'll come.' She crossed the room and flung her arms about him.

He examined her face. 'You've been weeping. What is this? What's been going on?' He turned to Silas, waiting for an explanation while placing a protective arm about Doreen.

She spoke hastily. 'It's nothing—just a personal matter. I'm OK now that you're here, Clive darling. Oh, I'm so glad to see you.'

Silas said in a dry tone, 'Isn't it time you made an introduction, Doreen?'

She flushed, suddenly becoming flustered. 'Oh—yes—Silas, this is Clive—a friend of mine from Sydney.'

The man gave a short laugh. 'More than a mere friend, I hope. Hell's teeth, baby—we've been living together for the last two years or more.'

'You mean in a *de facto* relationship?' Silas asked silkily.

'Yeah, that's what they call it. *De facto*. I mean—who needs to get married these days——?'

Doreen cut in hastily. 'How did you find me?'

'I got in touch with your old man, baby, and then I was lucky enough to get a lift to this—this Wilderness place.' He turned to Silas. 'Say, what's this white-water rafting I've heard about?' The question came eagerly.

Silas ignored it. Instead he said, 'I think you spoke of

taking Doreen home. Her car is out in the parking area.
I'm sure she's ready to go—*now*.' His voice held an
imperative note of dismissal.

'It won't take long for me to pack,' Doreen told Clive.
'You can help me.' She snatched his hand and almost
dragged him from the kitchen. It was the last Lucy was
to see of her.

Jean, who had remained in the doorway as an
interested spectator, spoke shyly to Silas. 'I'm so pleased
about you and Lucy, boss. As I left the room I heard
you say. . .' She smiled. 'So may I tell Mum?'

Lucy was suddenly panic-stricken. 'No—not a word
to anyone. He didn't *really* mean it—it was just a ploy to
be rid of Doreen.'

Silas spoke drily. 'It appears that I have some sorting
out to do. Close the door after you, Jean, and in the
meantime please keep it as a secret.' He waited until the
door was firmly shut, then he took Lucy in his arms
again. 'Now, then—what is this nonsense?' he
demanded, staring down into her face.

'I just find it almost impossible to believe——'

'I know the circumstances weren't the best, but, even
so, I'd like to know what makes you doubt my sincere
proposal of marriage.' His eyes narrowed as he studied
her face. 'Or is it that you yourself wish to withdraw
from the commitment?'

Her arms tightened about him. 'No—no, of course
not.' It was almost a cry of protest.

'Is it that you doubt that I love you?' he murmured.

'You've never told me,' she said in a low voice.

'Has it been necessary? Haven't you guessed? Haven't
women an intuition that is supposed to tell them these
things?'

'Mine has been buried beneath your determination to
remain free of the female species.'

'Then hear this, my dearest one—I love you. I love

you so much I can't live without you,' he whispered against her lips.

The words rang in her ears like bells heralding joy, and as the kiss ended she asked, 'So what happened to your previous determination to live without women?'

'I'm afraid it vanished along the main highway. It happened one day when I ran out of petrol and this girl came along. She had eyes as blue as cornflowers——'

'She's the one who is good at figures and has ability at the barbecue?' she asked pointedly, deciding to get all these aggravating niggles off her chest.

He laughed. 'Heaven give me strength. If I can't attend to my own accounts after years of accountancy I might as well go and jump in the river. As for the barbecue, even the guides can handle it in an emergency, but after the strenuous river trip I prefer them to be able to relax. I like to take care of my staff, just as I intend to take care of my wife—if the one I love will marry me.'

'Of course I'll marry you. Dearest Silas—did I happen to tell you I love you?' she queried shyly.

'I thought I'd never hear you say the words.' He kissed her with an ardour that left her breathless. As the kiss ended he said, 'Now, then, there's much to be done. First we'll tell Matt of our engagement, then give him the pleasure of telling the rest of the staff.'

'And tomorrow?' she queried, recalling that tomorrow was to have been a most dismal day, when she would leave Wilder's Wilderness and return to Wellington.

'Tomorrow, my dearest, we'll drive to Hastings to buy an engagement ring. After that we'll visit Bertha. I shall arrange for her to be transferred to a private hospital where she can have her own room with a TV and a phone beside the bed. I know she'd like that.'

'And then?' she asked dreamily, revelling in the feel of his chin against her forehead.

'Then I shall drive you to Wellington, where I'll meet your parents and inform your father you'll not be returning to the office. There will also be the matter of a marriage licence.'

Silas kissed her again and she was still in his arms when Ling walked into the room.

The sharp black eyes gleamed with interest as they took in the situation at once. 'Very interesting scene,' he commented. 'Has something been going on in my kitchen? That fellow you call Cupid has been flapping his wings and shooting his arrows?' The questions came politely.

'That's right, Ling,' Silas admitted. 'Lucy and I are to be married.'

Ling beamed. 'Congratulations, boss. I'm glad you take my advice. Didn't I tell you a woman in the bed is worth two at the table?'

Lucy blushed, but had to laugh as they went to find Matt. So Ling had been at Silas too, she thought.

Early the following month a radiant Lucy walked up the aisle on her father's arm. The small church was filled with relatives and friends, including the entire staff from the Wilderness, who were regarded as family.

Two of Lucy's school-mates, dressed in palest apricot, were bridesmaids, and when the bridal car arrived they were waiting in the entrance porch to make sure her veil cascaded over the gown of pearl-trimmed white lace.

Her hand trembled slightly as she place it on her father's arm, but when she heard the traditional strains of music announcing her arrival, and saw Silas looking extremely handsome as he waited at the end of the aisle, her nervousness fled.

Filled with love, she longed to run towards him, but controlled the impulse; then, when he came towards her with his hand outstretched, her heart felt swollen with joy.

After that she stood in a hazy dream, listening to the words that made them husband and wife.

Let

HARLEQUIN ROMANCE®
take you

BACK TO THE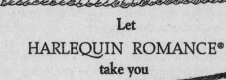

Come to the Tully T Ranch near Fortune, Texas
(a blink-and-you'll-miss-it cow town!).

Meet Evelina Pettit, better known as Evvie, a schoolteacher
from Houston who comes to help with the "Return to Good
Fortune" celebrations. *And meet* rancher Ryan Garrison. He
wants a wife—even though he doesn't believe in love. *Read*
Virginia Hart's THE PERFECT SCOUNDREL and watch
what happens when the schoolmarm meets the cowboy!

THE PERFECT SCOUNDREL is our next Back to the
Ranch title, available in March,
wherever Harlequin Books are sold.

RANCH10

HARLEQUIN®

Don't miss these Harlequin favorites by some of our most distinguished authors!
And now, you can receive a discount by ordering two or more titles!

HT#25409	THE NIGHT IN SHINING ARMOR by JoAnn Ross	$2.99	☐
HT#25471	LOVESTORM by JoAnn Ross	$2.99	☐
HP#11463	THE WEDDING by Emma Darcy	$2.89	☐
HP#11592	THE LAST GRAND PASSION by Emma Darcy	$2.99	☐
HR#03188	DOUBLY DELICIOUS by Emma Goldrick	$2.89	☐
HR#03248	SAFE IN MY HEART by Leigh Michaels	$2.89	☐
HS#70464	CHILDREN OF THE HEART by Sally Garrett	$3.25	☐
HS#70524	STRING OF MIRACLES by Sally Garrett	$3.39	☐
HS#70500	THE SILENCE OF MIDNIGHT by Karen Young	$3.39	☐
HI#22178	SCHOOL FOR SPIES by Vickie York	$2.79	☐
HI#22212	DANGEROUS VINTAGE by Laura Pender	$2.89	☐
HI#22219	TORCH JOB by Patricia Rosemoor	$2.89	☐
HAR#16459	MACKENZIE'S BABY by Anne McAllister	$3.39	☐
HAR#16466	A COWBOY FOR CHRISTMAS by Anne McAllister	$3.39	☐
HAR#16462	THE PIRATE AND HIS LADY by Margaret St. George	$3.39	☐
HAR#16477	THE LAST REAL MAN by Rebecca Flanders	$3.39	☐
HH#28704	A CORNER OF HEAVEN by Theresa Michaels	$3.99	☐
HH#28707	LIGHT ON THE MOUNTAIN by Maura Seger	$3.99	☐

Harlequin Promotional Titles

#83247	YESTERDAY COMES TOMORROW by Rebecca Flanders	$4.99	☐
#83257	MY VALENTINE 1993	$4.99	☐
	(short-story collection featuring Anne Stuart, Judith Arnold, Anne McAllister, Linda Randall Wisdom)		

(limited quantities available on certain titles)

	AMOUNT	$
DEDUCT:	10% DISCOUNT FOR 2+ BOOKS	$
ADD:	POSTAGE & HANDLING	$
	($1.00 for one book, 50¢ for each additional)	
	APPLICABLE TAXES*	$ _____
	TOTAL PAYABLE	$ _____
	(check or money order—please do not send cash)	

To order, complete this form and send it, along with a check or money order for the total above, payable to Harlequin Books, to: **In the U.S.:** 3010 Walden Avenue, P.O. Box 9047, Buffalo, NY 14269-9047; **In Canada:** P.O. Box 613, Fort Erie, Ontario, L2A 5X3.

Name: _____

Address: _____ City: _____

State/Prov.: _____ Zip/Postal Code: _____

*New York residents remit applicable sales taxes.
Canadian residents remit applicable GST and provincial taxes.

HBACK-JM

This Valentine's Day
give yourself something special. Something that's
just right for the most romantic day of the year.
Something that's all about love...

TWO FOR THE
*H*EART

Two brand-new stories in one volume!
THE PROPOSAL by Betty Neels,
a favorite author for almost twenty-five years
and
THE ENGAGEMENT by Ellen James,
a new author with a fast-growing readership
*Two brand-new stories that will satisfy,
charm and delight you!*

 HARLEQUIN ROMANCE®

*From the heart and for the heart—
especially on Valentine's Day....*
Available in February, wherever
Harlequin books are sold.

HRTFH